Center Stage

By
Bernadette Marie

5 Prince Publishing
Denver, Colorado
www.5princebooks.com

ISBN
This is a fictional work. The names, characters, incidents, places, and locations are solely the concepts and products of the author's imagination or are used to create a fictitious story and should not be construed as real.

5 PRINCE PUBLISHING AND BOOKS, LLC
PO Box 16507
Denver, CO 80216
www.5PrinceBooks.com
www.BernadetteMarie.com

Copyright © 2012 5 Prince Publishing and Books, LLC.
Bernadette Marie

Author Photo: Copyright ©2009 Damon Kappell/Studio 16
ISBN 13: 978-1-939217-15-8 ISBN 10: 1939217156

First Printing USA December 2012
5 PRINCE PUBLISHING AND BOOKS, LLC.

For Stan~
You have always been the spotlight shining down on me at Center Stage.

ACKNOWLEDGEMENTS

To my fabulous five—you make every day an adventure that I couldn't do without. You are my world!

To my amazing husband—20 years is only the beginning of this crazy life together. You have been an amazing source of inspiration.

To my sister—thank you for being "Bernadette's Sister" and for accepting that as a good thing. I would have lunch with you any day!

To my mom and dad—nothing would ever be possible without the early guidance from you. Thank you for letting me converse with the voices in my head and spend countless hours making piles on the tables with my words.

To Connie and Marie—Thank you for keeping me in order. I appreciate that more than you'll ever know.

To Anne—You've been invaluable! Without your preciseness this would never be done so wonderfully and on time!

To Amanda, Gina, and Kammee—Thank you for jumping in to the selfless task of beta reading for the masses! Your support is appreciated!

Dear Reader,

I would like to first thank you for keeping up with the Keller family. This series has been a joy to write and I look forward to continuing with the next set of Keller siblings—Eduardo, Clara, and Christian.

This eclectic family has brought a great deal of joy to so many of you and without your support it would never be possible to continue on.

In Center Stage, we follow up with our favorite construction foreman John Forrester. Now that Arianna Keller has moved back to Nashville there is no reason to avoid the sparks which have been flying between the two of them any longer—except Arianna is keeping a secret that could threaten the lives of her entire family.

As in every Keller family book, you will find this family coming together to support one another. But as always, I offer you a Happily Ever After—that's my motto.

Enjoy Center Stage! I know I enjoyed building it for you. And when you are done there is a sampling of things to come in the future. The first chapter of Eduardo's story, Lost and Found, is at the conclusion of this book.

Happy Reading!
Bernadette Marie

Center Stage

The Keller Family Series
Book Four

Chapter One

Arianna pushed down on the suitcase and forced the zipper to close. The rest of her apartment was packed and ready for movers, but she'd need all her clothes before her belongings arrived in Tennessee.

She looked around her small, New York apartment. It had been a good home to her for the past decade. She'd accomplished everything she'd wanted. When she'd moved there, it was to try her hand on the stages of Manhattan. She'd played in some dives and had worked her way up to leads on Broadway. She had a few commercials to her credit and had graced a few TV shows as an extra, but her love was still on stage. But now it was time to go home, back where her family was. Something would come together for her there. It always did.

Arianna looked at her watch. She had barely enough time to get to the airport. If there were any accidents backing up traffic, she'd miss her flight.

Her brother-in-law, Zach, had called and said her sister Regan had gone into labor with the couple's second baby. She figured she'd arrive just in time to get to hold the bundle of joy. Then in a few more weeks, her brother, Curtis, and his fiancée, Simone, would have their first child. She knew moving back to Tennessee was right, and getting to spoil new nieces and nephews was reason enough to be closer to home.

The flight had been miserable. Leaving New York in a January snowstorm always meant delays and aggravation. It was almost eight o'clock at night by the time the flight landed two hours late. Carlos would be livid if he'd been waiting at the airport the entire time.

She made it to baggage claim, retrieved her two pieces of luggage, and then scanned the area for her brother. There was no sign of him, or any member of her family, anywhere.

"I thought I'd missed you," the familiar voice behind her said.

She spun quickly to find John Forrester, Zach's most trusted building foreman, standing there.

"Missed me? Were you looking for me?"

"I have been sent to pick you up. Carlos and Madeline ended up with Tyler for the night."

Arianna narrowed her stare on him when he'd commented about her nephew. "I thought Mom was watching him while the baby was born."

"Well, it seems as though your family is going to grow quite a bit tonight. Regan is still in labor, and Curtis just took Simone in. She's having her baby today, too."

Arianna gasped. "Simone isn't due for two more weeks."

"Babies come when babies want to, and Emily thought she'd better be there for Simone." He picked up her suitcases, one in each hand. "C'mon, my truck isn't too far."

Who would have thought she'd get to be there for the birth of both babies in one night. God had blessed the

Keller family—that was for sure. Carlos and Madeline's kids were teenagers, and in the next few years, they would be off on adventures of their own. Eduardo, their eldest, was already working for Zach after school. Christian, their second son, was an all-star athlete—baseball, she thought. And Clara, well, Clara was a girl after her own heart. She was an accomplished musician on the acoustic guitar. And, boy, could that girl sing.

Regan and Zach's son, Tyler, was as anxious as any sixteen-month-old child could be for a new sibling. But Arianna figured he'd need the most spoiling from her to make everything just right.

As for her, she'd never wanted children. It just hadn't been in her plans. Her career had always been more important. She came and went as she wanted, carried on in any fashion she saw fit, and, of course, traveled the world.

But now Nashville, Tennessee called her back home. Perhaps she could share her talent with the world in some other way.

John led her to his truck in the adjoining parking lot. She was comfortable with John, she thought, as she walked behind him. They had been each other's dates to both of Carlos's weddings last year, and they had hit it off, as friends of course. They might have hit it off more, but he was very conscious of their age difference, even though she wasn't worried about the thirteen years between them. His ex-wife had burned him badly ten years ago, and it was clear he didn't trust any woman.

Not that she'd been looking for a man, but she often thought if John hadn't been so worried about everything, they might have had something. As it was, they could keep each other's company comfortably. Coming home with all her brothers and her sister being married, that might just be what she needed—someone to keep her company.

John's truck was probably one of the most beat up pickup trucks she'd ever had the displeasure of riding in, and she'd been born and raised in Tennessee—she knew bad pickup trucks. But that was John's character. If it still worked, there was no need to replace it.

He backed out of the parking lot and headed toward the highway. Also common with John, he didn't have much to say unless you started the conversation.

"So, how is the construction business?" she asked.

"Zach keeps me busy. That's for sure."

"I'll bet. Do you think he'll take some time off after the baby is born?"

John laughed. "Sure he will. He will work from his office at home."

Arianna followed suit and laughed too. That sounded like her brother-in-law.

She watched as John merged lanes. His tanned skin showed the many years that he'd worked in the elements. The deep lines around his eyes never made him look old, she thought, only distinguished. Arianna liked her men distinguished. Age on a man had never bothered her. Oh, if her parents knew about some of the men she'd dated in New York, they certainly might have had an opinion on the matter.

She must be feeling the pang of needing someone to connect with, she decided, because the thought of running her fingers through John's salt and pepper shaded hair was almost irresistible. But she denied herself the pleasure. He probably wouldn't take too kindly to the lunatic sister-in-law of his boss making a move on him.

The long flight and drive out to the hospital must have worn her out more than she'd thought. She woke to John's hand on her arm.

"We're here. If you hurry, you might not miss the show."

She rubbed her eyes. "Aren't you coming in?"

"Not my place to be. But I'll drop your bags off for you. I assume you're staying at your place?"

She nodded. One of the perks of keeping your house when you moved away, especially if you knew you'd be back. "Yes. Of course."

"That was a sound business decision to keep the house and rent it out. Benson, Benson, and Hart keep good care of it."

"I wouldn't expect anything different. I know I have a renter in the basement, too. Hope they don't make too much noise. I'm a day sleeper."

John smiled. "Oh, he's a good guy. He won't bother you."

Arianna nodded and looked up at the hospital where her brother worked as an emergency room doctor. "Guess I'd better go meet the newest members of this crazy family." She slid across the seat and placed a kiss on John's unshaven cheek. "Thanks for the ride. I'll take you out for pizza and a beer."

"Never could turn down a woman who offered up pizza and beer."

She opened the door and climbed out. He was just her kind of man.

The waiting room was full of Kellers, including Carlos and Madeline, who held a sleeping Tyler.

Carlos stood and greeted her with a hug when she walked into the room. "I thought you were babysitting him so he didn't have to hang out here."

"C'mon, what's better than meeting your baby brother or sister in the middle of the night and knowing this is the kid you get to beat on for the rest of your life?"

Arianna laughed as Clara rushed over and hugged her. "Auntie, I have a new song for you. I wrote it myself."

"And I bet it's the best song ever."

Arianna pulled her niece to her side. This was just what she'd needed—her family.

John opened the door to Arianna's house. He supposed he'd have to relinquish his key now that she was home. He shut the door and carried her bags to the bedroom at the top of the stairs. He didn't open the door. He knew it was empty, but still, it was her bedroom.

The house was dark and quiet; he'd miss that too. There hadn't been a renter upstairs for months; he'd had the house to himself. Oh, he kept to himself downstairs in the little apartment in the basement, but he'd enjoyed using the front door access and the kitchen from time to time. There was a grill on the back porch, which offered the perfect view of the sunset. He was sure Arianna wouldn't mind him cooking a steak or two for her, just for access to the porch.

John grabbed a beer from the refrigerator as he passed through the kitchen. He figured he'd better get his plugged in downstairs. It had been a saver on electricity since the one he had in his kitchen was old, and Arianna's kept the beer colder.

He started down the stairs to his little apartment. The door locked from her side, which kept the renters out of the house. He'd taken liberty with that since the house was empty, but certainly he wouldn't disrespect that rule when she came back home.

His small apartment was just the right size. He was a simple man who didn't need much—and who didn't have much since his ex-wife took everything he'd ever had. Ten years after she'd left him for another man, he still wondered what he'd ever seen in her. Well, he'd never make that mistake again. Women just weren't worth it. Most women, he corrected himself. His mind had been preoccupied with one woman in particular for months. And now he faced the dilemma of knowing she'd be living only feet from him.

The last thing he wanted was a relationship—platonic or just sexual. Relationships had never brought him anything but grief.

John sat down on his Lazy Boy recliner and turned on his big screen, flat panel TV. A man had to have his luxuries. He pulled from his imported beer and thought life was good.

But only a moment later, his mind wandered to Arianna. With her hair piled atop her head, her eyes dark from lack of sleep, and her ripped jeans, she'd still stirred him up more than he'd have liked.

Beer and pizza sounded like a great idea, but he wouldn't take her up on the offer until he knew they'd cemented their relationship as landlord/renter and friends—only friends.

CHAPTER TWO

The night dragged into early morning, and the entire Keller family still sat in the waiting room and waited. Carlos's head rested on Arianna's shoulder, and he held Tyler in his arms. Clara had taken Arianna's lap as a pillow, and she too was asleep.

Eduardo had been frantically texting on his phone until almost midnight, but she noticed that now he and Christian both had their feet propped up on the same table and their eyes were closed.

She seemed to be the only one awake, and she was happy that she was the only one to see her brother-in-law, Zach, walk into the room.

There was an unmistakable grin on his face, and his tired eyes shimmered. He gave her a quiet nod toward the room. She acknowledged with a similar nod, and then went about readjusting Clara and Carlos so that she could stand up.

Quickly she ran to her brother-in-law's waiting arms and gave him an enormous hug.

"She wanted to see you first," he whispered in her ear and then wrapped his arm around her waist and led her down the hall.

There was an excitement that buzzed through her. Regan had asked for her.

Regan and Arianna had been Kellers for nearly their entire lives. In fact, she didn't remember her life before the Kellers adopted her, but the fact remained, even before the Keller family, it was always her and Regan.

They'd always shared that bond, even when their parents changed and siblings were added.

Having Regan ask for her to meet her baby first gave Arianna a pride and joy that she figured could only be rivaled with having her own baby, and she had no desire for that.

Regan was propped up in bed and her new born bundle of joy was wrapped in her arms in a blanket.

Arianna moved quietly to the side of the bed and kissed her sister on the cheek.

"I want you to meet Spencer."

Regan handed her son to her, and Arianna fell in love. She'd done the same when she'd handed Tyler to her, too. The children of her siblings were her life. She wasn't sure she could be more blessed.

"Hello, Mr. Spencer. I'm Auntie Arianna. I'm in charge of spoiling you rotten."

Zach moved in beside her. "You're setting him up, you know."

"I know. But as I don't ever plan to have one of these, spoiling yours is my sole purpose in life. I think I've done a fairly good job with Carlos's kids, and Tyler seems to like me just fine."

He put his arm around her shoulders and gave her a squeeze. "It looks like he's very happy to have you as his auntie."

At that moment, the door flew open and Curtis stood there, frozen with his face paralyzed in what appeared to be a panic.

Regan sat up straighter and then quickly relaxed. "What's wrong? Simone? Is she okay?"

Curtis only nodded. "Girl."

Arianna watched as Regan's face softened. "You have a baby girl?"

Curtis nodded.

Arianna laughed. He was a trauma doctor stunned by the birth of his own child. "Congrats, Daddy."

Curtis wiped his hand over his head. "I think I should sit down."

Zach hurried to him. "Rookie. C'mon, let's go see this princess of yours before the rest of the family wakes up."

"Curtis." Arianna waited for him to turn toward her. "What is her name?"

"Oh. Yeah. Avery. Avery Emily."

"I'll be down there next to meet my niece."

He only nodded again and let Zach help him out of the room.

Regan laughed. "He's doomed. Absolutely doomed."

"We think Simone has him wrapped around her finger. Just wait until Avery needs something." She held Spencer's little hand. "I can't believe you both had your babies on the same day."

"That will be a special bond between them."

The door opened again, and this time their parents walked in with Tyler holding tightly to his grandmother's hand.

Regan reached her arms out to him and tears rolled down her cheeks as Tyler ran toward her. His grandmother helped him onto Regan's bed and she wrapped her arms around him. "Look, Tyler, you're a big brother."

Tyler lifted his head and looked at the baby in Arianna's arms.

"His name is Spencer," she told him as he rested his head on his mother's shoulder and quickly fell asleep.

Their mother held out her arms. "Let me see my grandson."

Arianna handed her nephew off to her mother and turned to hug her father. "I'm going to go meet my niece and then head home. I'm exhausted."

"Thank you for being here," Regan whispered as not to stir Tyler or Spencer.

"I wouldn't have missed it for the world. I'm very lucky to have made it for both."

Arianna walked out to the hallway and followed the sounds of her brother's voice.

Curtis was seated in a chair, his arms resting on his knees, and Zach hovered over him with a glass of water.

The sight nearly had her busting out in laughter.

Simone shook her head. "You would think he did all the work."

Arianna wondered if Simone had seen a mirror. Her long, black tresses were matted down to her skin. Her face was still flush, and her eyes were bloodshot. However, Arianna thought she'd never looked better.

She walked to Simone's bedside and took her first look at her beautiful niece. "Hello, Avery."

"Is she not the most beautiful girl in the world?"

"She just might be. May I hold her?"

Simone was not as quick to give up her first child to her doting auntie as Regan was, and that was expected.

"Oh, Simone, she is just wonderful." She looked up at Curtis who was now sitting upright. "You can mend severed limbs, but a baby does you in?"

"Don't give me your grief. You weren't here."

She looked down at Simone. "Was it that bad?"

"They have drugs for mothers, not for fathers."

Arianna laughed, but kept it quiet. "I never thought you were a wimp."

"In my defense," he said as he stood, "I didn't like that it caused her pain. I caused her that pain."

Arianna felt the sting of tears now. Her brother had sincerely meant what he said, and it moved her.

She gave Avery a kiss on the top of her head and handed her back to Simone.

"Congratulations. I'm so very happy for you."

It was six o'clock in the morning when Carlos dropped Arianna off at her house. She was sure that was the longest day of her life, and she knew long days.

She pushed open the door to her house and looked around. Whose stupid idea had it been to rent out the house and get rid of the furniture? Oh, yeah, hers.

The door closed behind her and she turned to lock it. Her footsteps echoed as she walked toward the kitchen. At that moment, she wished she'd stopped by McDonald's for a coffee. And, in that instant, she realized not only would her coffee maker be another few days out from arriving, but she had no bed.

Carlos certainly wasn't going to turn around and head back to pick her up and take her to his house. And she was so tired she didn't even care. She'd sleep on the pile of clothes in her suitcase if she had to.

With that thought, she wondered where John had left her suitcase. She walked toward the stairs and could see it at the top. How generous of him to have carried it up because, at this point, she was so tired she didn't think she could have made it.

She climbed the stairs slowly. When she reached her bedroom, she noticed the door was open and someone had taken the time to put a blow up bed in there and make it up with sheets and blankets.

A chair sat next to the bed with a lamp, a small digital clock, and a note.

She walked in and picked up the note.

I realized you didn't have any furniture. This bed is yours for as long as you'd like. I also left some beer in the fridge and a cold pizza. John.

She held the note to her chest and breathed in. Could he be more amazing?

She looked down at the note again and ran her finger over the words.

He'd been thinking of her enough to do something so thoughtful. Was it possible he'd been thinking of her as much as she'd been thinking about him? Perhaps—but had he been thinking the same thoughts. Arianna knew her thoughts had kept her up nights in need of a cold shower.

Her stomach grumbled. As much as she'd like to just fall into the bed covered in John's sheets, she really wanted a piece of that pizza, and perhaps a beer would help her fall asleep. After all, her body was so tired it wouldn't know it was only six-thirty in the morning.

CHAPTER THREE

John scrubbed his hand over his face and zipped up his coat. The only part about working construction that he didn't like was that damn trailer he called an office.

In the summer he baked, and in the winter he froze. It didn't really matter if you had air conditioning or heat. The temperatures just got to a man once in a while.

The door opened, and he looked up. He hadn't expected to see a friendly face, and he was ready to throw his frozen mug of coffee at the person who let more cold in.

"Zach Benson, what are you doing here? You're on maternity leave, and my guess is your assistant doesn't know you're here or she'd be dragging you back to your wife."

Zach laughed and held his hand out to him. "Let's just say I came by with photos of my new son."

John shook his hand. "Nice way to make an excuse to check on the build."

"Whatever it takes." Zach pulled his iPhone from his pocket and brought up the picture. He handed it to John. "There are my boys. His name is Spencer."

"Congratulations, my friend. He looks healthy."

"He is. Tyler isn't so sure of him, but something tells me they'll be pals soon enough."

John handed him back his phone. "They're close enough Tyler will never remember not having Spencer around."

Zach gave a glance at the plans on the wall. "Looks like you're still on time and under budget."

"I don't run builds any other way."

"From the seat I sit in, I thank you for that." Zach slid his phone back into his pocket and bundled up his coat. "So how was Arianna this morning?"

"I didn't see her. I got here at six, and she still wasn't at the house."

"Things could get very cozy with you two living within feet of each other."

"I'm sure they could, but they won't. I respect your sister-in-law. She's safe with me around."

Zach nodded. "You do know I get my share of gossip. Regan and Arianna are very tight."

"And there is gossip where I'm concerned?"

"Just that Arianna took a liking to you."

"Well, she's a nice girl. Trust me, the last thing she needs is some old man, and I certainly don't plan to hit the dating pool again."

Zach shrugged. "At least she'll have you close."

He turned and left the office, and John rubbed the tension from his temples. He guessed it was time to find a new place to live.

It was past four in the afternoon when Arianna finally woke. She couldn't remember the last time she'd slept that long. But she needed it.

For the past fifteen years she'd been burning the candle at both ends trying to make a name for herself. She'd done that, but there had to be more.

She rolled off the air mattress John had left her and headed downstairs for another piece of cold pizza. Perhaps she could arrange for someone to give her a lift to her sister's house to pick up the car she kept there. There would need to be some groceries purchased. After all, a woman couldn't live for long on cold pizza and beer.

By five o'clock she'd showered and changed her clothes. She made the little bed on the floor and arranged her suitcase just right. Housekeeping was easy if you only had one bed and one suitcase.

She pulled her phone from her pocket to call her brother when the doorbell rang. She hurried down the stairs to the door, and when she opened it, she certainly wasn't disappointed. There stood John with a bag of groceries in his arms.

"I knew you didn't have anything in your fridge yet so I brought a few staples." He handed her the bag.

"How is it that in two days you've become my knight in shining armor."

"I come with gray hair only, no armor."

There was a flirtatious flutter in her, and it was going to surface. She couldn't help it. The man did something to her.

"Some women find gray very sexy," she said as she turned and walked toward the kitchen. "C'mon in for a bit."

He shut the door and followed her.

She watched him walk slowly through the living room. She'd ruffled his feathers. But what she'd like to do is ruffle that hair he was complaining about.

She opened the door to the refrigerator and ducked behind it to keep her smile hidden. She was desperate. Maybe she should head to a bar, pick up a guy, and bring him home for a bounce on the air mattress. John wouldn't be the guy to take her up on such, but he was certainly stirring her up.

"I figured you could use a ride to your sister's house to get your car."

Arianna closed the door to the refrigerator and nodded. "I had just picked up my phone to call Carlos and ask him to come get me when you showed up. So, yes, I could absolutely use a ride."

"Then I'm your guy."

He most certainly was.

She grabbed her coat and locked the front door. She followed him to the beat up truck in the driveway. "How come Zach doesn't give you a company truck?"

John opened the door for her and waited for her to climb in. "I have one." He shut the door and walked around to the other side.

"Then why don't you drive it? This truck has to be as old as Tennessee."

He gave a shrug and started the engine. It protested and finally growled into commission. "I never needed anything better. My tools are in the back, my name is on the title, and she's paid for. What more does a guy need?"

"How about dinner?"

He turned and looked at her, his eyes questioning.

"Let me take you to dinner. This is the second time in two days you've come to my rescue." She shook her head. "No, wait, the fourth."

"Fourth?"

"I forgot to thank you for the bed."

He chuckled. "My pleasure. Figured you'd rather have something to sleep on than the floor."

"It was very appreciated. And thank you for the groceries."

"My pleasure."

She clasped her hands together and put them in her lap. She hoped the heater would start warming up. "So what do you say? Dinner?"

He bit down on his lip, and she figured he was going to turn her down. John Forrester wasn't one to get mixed up with a woman, and here she was offering dinner. Oh, she was going to make him her pet project. She'd have her way with the man if it killed her, just to say she'd broken him.

"I suppose I could eat. What did you have in mind?"

"Bar-b-que."

"Missed home, huh?"

"Absolutely."

He wasn't sure what he was doing driving her downtown for dinner. He should have told her no. It was bad enough he hadn't found a new apartment yet and he was going to have to tell her he lived in the same house, and living under the same roof didn't seem like a sound idea. The woman had him thinking thoughts he hadn't thought in years. There was no way he was getting involved with the boss's sister-in-law, for one, and he didn't need another woman in his life. One had been enough.

John pulled the truck into the lot at Steve's BBQ Pit and Beer. Immediately Arianna let out a snort.

"Regan told me about this place."

"Did she?" He opened his door and climbed out. He would have helped her out of the truck, but she was already closing the door and walking toward the restaurant. His ex-wife would have needed the pampering, but not this one. She was as strong headed as they came.

"I think this was the first place Zach brought her when he was trying to make his moves on her."

John stopped walking. He'd forgotten about that. He sure hoped Arianna wasn't thinking the same thing.

She turned back and looked at him. "You comin'?"

He gave her a nod and followed her inside.

The greeter at the front walked them to a booth in the corner. He'd thought about requesting two seats at the bar, but Arianna bounced into the booth and pulled out a menu.

"I haven't had good ribs in a long time."

"This is the place to get them."

When the waitress came to the table, they each ordered a beer and placed their dinner order. Arianna tucked the menu back into its place behind the salt and pepper shakers, laced her hands on the table, and looked right at him.

"So, anything new since we last dated?"

John cleared his throat and wished his beer would arrive quickly. His mouth had gone dry.

"Dated?"

"Just kidding." She sat back against the booth. "Why are you all worked up having me around?"

"Am I? I didn't notice."

She nodded. "C'mon, I didn't make any plays on you at Carlos's last wedding. We just had a good time."

"We did."

The waitress set their beers down, and John took in after his. Of course he'd only have one if he was driving, but he might have to have an entire six-pack when he got home.

"I'm glad Madeline and Carlos are back together. I liked Kathy, but Madeline was the one for him always."

"And Curtis and Simone? When are they getting married?"

"When she can fit into a dress again." She leaned over the table on her elbows. "What do ya say? Be my date?"

"People will start to talk."

"Let 'em." She leaned back and took a sip from her beer. "One thing you won't find me doing is getting married and having babies."

He felt his body heat rise. "Really? All these babies being born and you're not getting baby fever?"

She shook her head. "No way. I have other plans in my life."

"Like what?"

She shrugged. "I think I'd like to teach theater. Maybe even own a theater someday. You know, community theater. Perhaps write some plays."

He nodded slowly.

Arianna took another sip of her beer. "You think it's stupid, don't you?"

"Not in the least."

In fact, he knew of a theater that was slated for demolition if it wasn't purchased. He'd look into it and see if it was worth saving. Then maybe he'd tell her about it. After all, she seemed safe enough. She didn't want marriage or kids. Maybe they could just share a meal and a beer after all. Then again, what came after that?

CHAPTER FOUR

It was later than John had thought when he finally pulled up to Zach's house. Zach's office light was on. He wanted to laugh at the man. He was brought up all business, and it didn't seem as though much had changed, but John knew the family he was building was more important than any business venture. He'd seen it in Zach's eyes the moment he'd fallen in love and again when Alexander Hamilton had approached them at a business meeting and threatened Regan.

John's fingers tensed around the steering wheel. Zach would go to the ends of the world to protect his wife and, now, his children. Losing multi-million dollar builds didn't matter when you loved someone.

Zach loved what he did. But he loved his family more.

John stopped the truck and turned off the engine.

Arianna looked at the house and then back at him. "Thank you for the ride and for dinner."

John gave her a slow nod. "My pleasure."

"But I still owe you a meal. I think I had said I was taking you out."

"I'm very southern. I don't know if I'm going to be able to let you pay for my meal."

Arianna let out a grunt and shook her head. "Get over it, Forrester," she said as she zipped up her coat.

"I'll do my best." He opened his door. "I'll get the door."

He shut his door behind him and walked around the front of the truck to the other side. She already had it open when he reached for the handle.

"You are a good-ole-boy, aren't ya?"

"I try." He held out his hand for her to take as she climbed out of his old truck.

When she landed on the ground, she was close enough that he could feel the heat from her body. He deliberately took a step back.

"Do you want me to wait for you and follow you back to your house?"

Arianna laughed and rested her hand on his chest. He was glad he had a heavy coat on so she wouldn't feel the rise in his heart beat when she'd touched him.

She shook her head. "I've been around these roads my whole life. I'll be fine." Arianna lifted herself up on the balls of her feet and planted a kiss on his cheek. "Thanks again for saving me all the time."

He cleared his throat and tried to clear his mind. "Always my pleasure."

Zach opened the front door and stepped out onto the porch. "Are you two going to make out in my drive?"

Arianna laughed easily again. "I certainly wouldn't do that here if I were. I can think of a million other places to be making out." She walked toward the house and turned back to John. "Thanks again. I'm going to go kiss Tyler."

"Don't wake him up," Zach warned.

"I promise." And she was gone.

Zach walked down the steps, his arms crossed over his chest to obviously fight off the chill, and toward John.

"Did you take her out on her first night back?"

"Just offered her a ride out here is all. We did catch a bite to eat. She had a hankering for bar-b-que."

Zach's eyebrows rose. "Steve's."

"Only place to go, right?"

"Right." He sincerely hoped Zach wasn't reading anything into his dinner with Arianna. He didn't need Zach or Regan filling her head with any ideas.

Arianna drove the dark roads back to town. The image of John and Zach standing in the drive talking had burned into her mind. She'd watched them from Tyler's bedroom window. There was a comfort between the two men, much like that of her brothers when they spoke. She couldn't help but wonder what they were talking about. Did they talk about her?

It was silly to think about, really. She didn't come home to find a man. She came home because she didn't feel safe in New York anymore, and she didn't feel as though her family in Nashville was safe either.

Arianna wiped the back of her hand over her forehead. The decision to move back to Nashville had been quick. She'd quit her job and had her things packed within two weeks. After all, when you hear a big investor with the theater wants to meet you and then are suddenly face to face, alone in the dressing room, with the man who tried to murder your sister and her baby, panic takes over.

She turned down the road that would take her home and had to force herself to slow down. It was as if she couldn't lock herself in her house fast enough.

She finally pulled into the driveway, threw the car in park, and sat there.

How could she have ever known Alexander Hamilton was the man coming to meet her? Never, in her wildest dreams, would she have thought he'd show his face again.

Arianna had mixed emotions about Curtis telling Alexander that Regan had died after the bastard had beaten her when she was pregnant with his child. She'd always been afraid it would come back to haunt them. Arianna thought they should have had him turned in, thrown in jail, or even murdered.

But it hadn't happened her way, and eventually Alexander Hamilton crossed paths with Regan. He knew they'd lied to him, and he wanted to know where the baby was.

Arianna sucked in a breath. She'd kept the secret of the baby. She had told him to his face that the baby had died, but she wasn't sure he had bought it—and she wasn't even sure he had cared. Alexander Hamilton was all about power, and when he'd approached her, he'd had power over her. But what she feared was that he'd come that close to her so what would stop him from coming to Nashville?

Zach would always protect Regan, but as her older sister, she felt the need to be there. Family was family, and you took care of your own. That was exactly what Arianna would do.

She took her keys and unlocked the glove compartment of her car. From inside, she pulled out the gun she'd kept there since she'd last lived in Nashville. She was sure Regan didn't even know it was in there, or she certainly wouldn't have let her keep it there.

Arianna slid it into her purse and stepped out of her car. She could see the lights from the basement windows, illuminated in the dark. Tomorrow she would make a point to meet her tenant. Tonight she was going to climb into that silly bed that John had left for her and get a good night's sleep.

Her furniture should arrive tomorrow. She'd need all the strength she could muster to get everything back in place just like she liked it.

John turned down the volume on his television when he heard the footsteps upstairs. She was home.

It was stupid that he'd even worried about her, but he considered her a friend. Friends worried.

He clicked off the old M*A*S*H episode and pushed himself up from his chair. He threw his beer bottle in the recycle bin and headed to bed. Saturdays were as busy in construction as any other day. He should have been in bed hours ago. The thought didn't settle well with him. If it hadn't been for worrying about Arianna so much, he'd have been in bed at a reasonable time. Instead he was having ribs and beer and taking drives out to Zach's. Just because he was single and willing to help didn't mean he'd intended to be her knight in shining armor.

He pulled off his T-shirt and threw it in the hamper, then pulled back the sheets on his bed and climbed in. He hadn't gotten much sleep last night, and he doubted he'd get much more knowing she was just upstairs.

The thought of Alexander Hamilton's face had kept Arianna awake most of the night. She didn't want it to seem as though she were running, but inside she couldn't help but feel that way. Sure, she was certainly strong enough when it had been Regan who had been haunted by the man, but now he'd entered her world. It was hard to feel as strong when she felt so vulnerable.

She looked at the little clock on the chair at the edge of the bed. It was only five-thirty in the morning and still dark outside. It had been a very long time since she'd seen this side of early morning, but if she went back to sleep, she just might have another nightmare.

Arianna rolled out of the bed and shuffled her way downstairs. It wasn't until she was standing, blurry eyed, in front of the empty kitchen counter that she remembered there wasn't a coffeemaker yet. She let out a long groan. The movers weren't supposed to arrive until two. There'd better be a Starbucks at the end of the street.

She turned from the counter and looked out the window over the sink. Not even a hint of orange graced the sky line yet. What the hell was she doing up?

Just as she started to turn away, she turned back. Something else caught her eye. The old, red, beat up Ford pickup truck she'd grown to loathe and love was parked out back by the garage.

She leaned up on the counter to look out into the yard. She didn't see John.

Arianna hurried to the front door, pulled it open and looked out front. He wasn't there either.

Now why would he park his truck at her house?

She heard the door that went from the small basement apartment to the outside open and shut. She'd get her first glimpse of her tenant. It was a little bit of a surprise when she saw John walking up the steps with a mug of coffee in his hands.

She hurried to the back door and stepped out to the porch. "What are you doing here this early?"

His head snapped up, obviously surprised to have someone talking to him in the early morning from the porch.

"You're up early," he said, his voice rough.

"Couldn't sleep. Are you working on something already?"

"Off to the build."

She shook her head and started for the stairs. "No. I meant here. Is something wrong with the apartment downstairs?"

"Nope. It's a nice, little place."

She could feel herself tense the closer she got to him. "No. Is there a leak or wiring problem or something?"

He only shook his head.

She dropped her shoulders. "Did you sleep here last night?"

His eyebrows drew together. "Yes," he said slow and drawn out.

She didn't expect that short, little word to rattle her. She swallowed hard. "Oh. You did." She stepped back. "So you're seeing someone?"

He looked her over as though he thought she'd lost her mind. "I think you need some coffee. Want some?"

"Coffee?"

"Yep." He started back down the steps to the door of the apartment.

Was he seriously going to take her into the apartment of the tenant he was sleeping with? It was six in the morning. She wasn't dressed. This wasn't how she wanted to meet the person who would be sending her rent checks. Nor did she like the fact that thinking about John with someone else was eating her up. This man was just an acquaintance, not the man fated to be hers. They'd gone to two weddings together. He took her to dinner and gave her a few rides. That does not signify that he wanted to spend the rest of his life with her—or expected to.

But before she could protest, he had the door open and had walked inside.

Arianna stood at the threshold and looked inside. This wasn't an apartment of any woman. It was dark not only because it was so darn early, but because it was decorated in dark hues. She hadn't remembered the space ever looking so nice.

The walls had been painted in browns and greens, and did it have hard wood flooring before? It must have. Who would just put that kind of thing into a rented apartment?

There was a small, leather couch under the two windows and a big Lazy Boy recliner with a small end table next to it. Both sat facing an enormous, out-of-place-in-such-a-small-space TV.

She could hear John in the tiny kitchen filling a mug with coffee, and she'd forever be grateful for that. When he came back into the room, he handed it to her.

"Thank you."

"You look like you can use it."

She nodded and enjoyed the warmth of the mug against the palms of her hand. "I take it that it's not some woman who lives here."

"Nope."

"But you didn't mention that you lived here."

"Sure didn't."

His short answers were frustrating. "But you do?"

"Yep."

"You're my nice guy tenant you told me about?"

"Yep."

What was she supposed to say to that? "Okay. Well, it's nice to know I'm in good hands then."

He nodded again, but this time with a glance at his watch. "You're welcome to more coffee if you'd like. I have to get to work."

"Oh, sure." She turned toward the door and then turned back to him, again standing very near to him. "You wouldn't object to me taking the coffee pot upstairs with me, would you? Mine won't arrive for a few more hours."

Arianna hurried up the cold, back stairs with his coffee pot in her arms and waved to him as he pulled out of the back drive. She disappeared into the house, and he sat there watching her figure move in the kitchen window.

It had been a long time since he'd see a woman, her hair mussed from sleep, in flannel pajama bottoms and an old T-shirt. The sight had stirred him immensely.

A pang in his chest let him know he'd missed having someone tell him goodbye in the mornings.

Common sense quickly jolted him back into place. There had been a reason he hadn't had a woman in his life regularly to tell him goodbye in the mornings. He needed to remember that.

But the image of Arianna, fresh from sleep, continued to play in his head as he drove to the site. Perhaps he'd try to wrap things up early today and head back to help her move furniture around. That would be the neighborly thing to do.

CHAPTER FIVE

What good were movers who literally dropped your furniture and boxes off and then ran as fast as they could? Arianna thought they'd help a little more.

She gathered her hair with her hands and then let it drop down around her shoulders as she looked at the mess in the once empty house. How did she have all of this stuff in one apartment?

The coffeemaker. She was going to dig through the boxes and find that stupid coffeemaker first, even if the thought of sharing one with John was appealing.

She moved boxes around the kitchen until she came to the one she knew must have the coffeemaker buried in it. Bent over at the waist, she reached into the box when she heard the knocking on the back door.

Her head snapped up out of the box and she spun around, nearly falling into the box. There stood John at the back door with the most adorable grin on his face.

Arianna wasn't sure if it was endearing or one of those quirks that was going to piss her off.

She pushed through boxes to get to the door and flung it open.

She fisted her hands on her hips. "What are you grinning at?"

"You're supposed to bend at the knees, not at the waist."

"Oh, you didn't like my ass up in the air?"

The comment was meant to be a bit snotty, but when she saw the flush in his cheeks and his eyes opened wide, she knew she'd caught him on exactly what he'd been grinning about.

John cleared his throat. "I cut out of work a little early to help you. If you need it."

Arianna grabbed his arm and twisted it just enough so she could look at his watch. "It is five o'clock. You call this getting out of work early?"

He shrugged. "Yeah. Stopped and looked at a building on my way home."

"Something new?"

"Maybe." He scratched his head. "You want a beer?"

Arianna let out a sigh. "I'd love one."

John took the steps down to his place slowly. He needed to clear his head.

What was it about Arianna Keller that made him do ridiculous things? He had been looking at her ass in the air, just as she'd hinted. That wasn't his way. He didn't find it amusing when the guys on site did it either.

And then there was that building he'd been looking at. The Rockwell Theater on the edge of town was slated to be torn down if it wasn't renovated. All he could think about was helping Arianna fix it up.

He rubbed the back of his neck as he walked into the kitchen. It was already getting complicated. He should drop the whole thing, sit down in his chair, and watch some sports on ESPN. After all, that was why he had that enormous TV. Sports and MythBusters—explosions were always better in high-definition.

He could hear boxes slide across the floor. A glance at his TV made him feel guilty. He pulled four beers out of the refrigerator and stood there with the door open.

Alone in his little space wasn't where he wanted to be. He wanted to be upstairs with her. Damn it!

The sound of feet on the stairs which led to the inside door of his apartment had his attention. Then there was a knock on the door. He walked across the room.

"Yes?"

"Can I open this?" Her voice was muffled from the other side.

"The door?"

"Yes."

"Why?" How silly was it they were yelling through it? He unlocked his side. "My side is unlocked. Unlock your side."

He heard the bold click, and Arianna pushed it open. "Cool." She looked around the kitchen where he stood with four beers in his arms.

"You shouldn't keep that door unlocked."

The corner of her mouth lifted into a grin. "Are you afraid I might sneak down and attack you?"

There she went again, stirring him up. "No." He shook his head. "What did you need?"

"Stupid question, but do you have a hammer, a screwdriver, and a wrench?"

"No."

Her nose crinkled in the most amusing and cute way, but he kept his lips pursed and forced himself not to smile.

"Oh. I just thought…" She was flustered.

"I was kidding. Of course I have those. They are in my truck. Here." He handed her the beers. "I'll go out and get them. You take these upstairs."

Arianna nodded, took the beers, and started up the steps which led to her own kitchen.

"Stop looking at my ass, Forrester."

Guilt dropped like a lead balloon into the pit of his stomach. Again, that was exactly what he'd been doing.

When he walked through her back door, Arianna was on the floor going through a box. The contents were spread all over the floor.

"Shouldn't you get your furniture in its place first, and then sort through the boxes?"

"I packed in a hurry. The boxes are mixed."

"What needs to be fixed?"

Arianna looked at him with a look of confusion clouding her eyes, but when he shook his hammer in his hand, she bolted up to her feet.

"Oh, yeah. The bed needs to be assembled."

Arianna started up the stairs to her bedroom, but John took a slower pace. He'd felt guilty enough putting the air mattress in there. He wasn't sure he wanted to be in her bedroom.

When he reached the top of the stairs, he heard her moving boxes around. As he walked through the door, a pillow flew his way and he was merely quick enough to catch it before it hit him in the face.

"You seem out of sorts tonight," Arianna said as she kicked a box into the corner.

"Do I?"

"Long day at the office, dear?"

Oh, she was playing with fire, and he was afraid he was the one getting burned in the process.

"It was a good day. Are these all the pieces?" He nodded toward the wall where the bed was stacked up.

"Yep. I want to sleep in my own bed tonight. I love that you set up the air mattress, but two nights is long enough. If we don't get this together soon, I might have to sleep in your bed."

She'd turned to gather another box in her arms and throw it in the corner, but he stood there with his mouth hung open, trying to make his heart beat normal.

He'd better get to work on that bed. There was no need to have Zach's sister-in-law making comments like that and getting him all worked up.

One thing John would say, after nearly forty-five minutes of piecing together the bed, they were a good team. Arianna was a strong woman, physically. She never minded lifting something or doing the hard work, where most women would have grunted or complained.

"Looks like one sturdy bed," John complimented, giving it a shake.

"Yes, well, those stupid movers put all the mattresses in the other room. So now I have to lug them over."

"I'm here to help."

"Good. And this time I promise to repay you, and you'll let me buy you dinner."

John tucked his thumbs into his front pockets. "You're determined to do that, huh?"

"I am."

"You know what sounds good? A steak on your grill."

Her eyes opened wide. "I am not a good cook. Your steak is going to end up a burnt brick."

He laughed. "I'll let you buy 'em. I'll grill 'em."

"Let's get this bed together first. Then we can make some deals."

She walked past him, leaving her scent in her wake.

The mattresses were flat on the floor, which he knew would be a bitch to get up especially since they were king-sized mattresses. From the looks of them, she'd spared no expense, just as the heavy oak bed.

"We'd be best to attack them from one side, lift vertically, and then we can push them out the door."

"Once we get over the stupid box springs." She looked around the room. "I don't remember this room being so small."

"I think your mattresses are just that big."

She laughed. "Pretty sad for a single gal, huh?"

"Space when you sleep is very important."

"I sleep on one edge. Only one edge. When I wake up, all I have to do is pull up the cover on that side."

This time he laughed. "I nearly have to start from scratch every morning. No wonder my wife left me. I must be a maniac when I sleep."

"Hmmmm." She turned as he looked at her, acknowledging the low hum that had resonated from her.

"C'mon. That cow ain't gonna get here on its own. Let's get this put together."

John bent his knees and took his position. Arianna watched him and then bent over at the waist and took her position, after a very obvious butt shake. When he felt the heat rise in his cheeks, he knew she'd seen it by the grin that settled on her lips. Then she bent at the knees, and together they hefted the heavy mattress onto its end.

They'd managed to clear it from the box springs and push it to her bedroom. They set it up against the wall and repeated the process for the box springs.

With the box springs in place, they pushed the mattress to the edge of the bed and gave it a hefty push, letting it fall.

"Now get on that side and pull while I push it into place," he said.

Arianna grabbed hold of the edge of the mattress, and John gave it an enormous shove that sent the mattress across the bed and right into Arianna's gut, causing her to slip and fall to the hardwood floor.

"God, are you okay?" He hurried around the bed.

There she was flat on the floor, holding her elbow, and laughing.

"You're not hurt, are you?"

"Just my pride, my ass, and my elbow."

He knelt down and took her arm. She winced as he straightened it.

"Looks okay."

She bent her arm and tried to look. "Eh, nothing to write home about."

"C'mon." He stood and held out his hands to help her up. She took hold of his hand and he pulled her up, sending her entire body slamming into him.

John's balance shifted and sent him back to the bed, pulling her down with him.

"We suck at this," she said laughing. Her dark curls shadowed her face as she looked down at him, pinned beneath her.

"Huh." What else could he say when the most beautiful woman he'd ever know had him on her bed, her body pressed against.

Her eyes changed the longer he was silent. This was no longer just a moment where he was helping her put her home back together. This was a moment he'd thought of a million times and swore he'd never take advantage of, but with her breath growing heavier the longer she stared down at him, he had no choice.

His hand went to her hair, and his fingers tangled in the curls. He pulled her down until their lips were just a breath apart. She looked into his eyes. A want—a need—glossed over them, and he knew, in that moment, they weren't leaving to get steak.

John's fingers pulled at her hair as his mouth opened to hers. Oh, she'd waited for this moment for months, though she'd never expected him to make the first move.

His lips, rough from the cold and wind, scraped against hers. His tongue sought hers out, and his hand pressed against the small of her back.

It had been so long since a man had such an urgency to kiss her that her head spun. Maybe it wasn't the time frame at all, maybe it was the man. This man.

John pulled at her shirt until he broke the kiss to pull it over her head. But his lips were back to hers in an instant.

She began a quick assault on the buttons of his red, flannel shirt. The fabric spread open revealing a white T-shirt beneath.

Arianna pushed the shirt from his chest, and with her mouth still engaged hungrily in the kiss that was rocking her entire insides, she pulled the shirt from his arms and then yanked the T-shirt over his head.

Beneath her hands lay muscles sculpted from years of manual labor. Sparse, gray hair shimmered over his chest.

She ran her hand over his skin and felt his heart beat beneath her fingertips.

John pushed back on the bed, his hands making quick work of her bra clasp as she tried to manage the button on his jeans.

No longer could she feel the draft of cold she'd felt in the room earlier. Her skin was heating up under his touch.

Before she'd managed to release the button on his pants, he'd freed her of hers and she lay there naked, vulnerable, and ready.

"You're beautiful." His eyes skimmed over her body.

There had been times, in similar situations, where she was uncomfortable and wanted to hide, but not with John. There was something in the way he looked at her—gazed at her—which made her want more.

His mouth went to her neck and trailed to her breast. She arched against him, and her nails dug into his skin.

He moved back to her neck and then to her ear. "I'm having a great deal of guilt that I want to make love to you."

"Why?" she asked breathlessly.

"You're young."

She knew she shouldn't laugh, but there was no way around it. "I'm almost forty."

"Much younger than me."

She couldn't help but pull back. "How much younger?" Not that it mattered. The man had driven her crazy for months, and she wanted this more than anything. "No." She nipped his lips with her teeth. "It doesn't matter. I've wanted this since Carlos's first wedding. So don't stop now."

He brushed a kiss down her neck. "I'm not prepared for this. I certainly didn't think I'd end up with you under me."

"John," she said as she cupped his face in her hands. "Trust me. I'm taken care of. I want this. And bless you, but I'm not young. So if you don't hurry, I'm liable to roll you over and take control of this situation."

The humor was back in his eyes and that made him even sexier, which she didn't think that was possible.

His mouth was back on hers, hot, hungry, and tantalizing her skin as he worked his lips and tongue over her body. Somehow his pants had been worked off, and it was just them, skin to skin, on her mattress starting a fire that she could only hope would never burn out.

Arianna's heart pounded in her chest. Strands of her hair stuck to her sweaty face, and John's arms were wrapped around her, his rapid breath warm against her neck.

They had done it—broke that sacred bond of growing friendship and traded it for hot, sweaty, amazing sex.

"I don't know how old you think you are, but," she said, trying to catch her breath, "you're absolutely amazing."

"I'm glad you think so."

She rolled over so they were face to face. He brushed away the strands of hair from her face. "You didn't want to do this, did you?"

"Oh, hell, I wanted to do it. I just didn't think it was the right thing to do. And it kinda puts us in a strange situation, doesn't it?"

"Not at all. Your rent just went up. Now you don't have to feel guilty."

He laughed as he interlaced their fingers. "What will your sister think?"

"Are you going to tell her?"

He adjusted to look at her. "I assumed you would."

"Well, of course I will, in time." She pressed a kiss to his lips. "But I don't tell her everything."

"I don't believe you."

She turned away again and pressed against him, wrapping his arm around her. No, he was wrong. She certainly didn't tell her sister everything. Regan had no idea what had made her come back to Nashville.

CHAPTER SIX

Arianna had fallen asleep wrapped in John's arms, atop her bare mattress with only his flannel shirt draped over both of them. When she'd awaken, he was propped up on his elbow staring down at her.

"You didn't run away." She rolled against him, resting her cheek against his chest.

"Did you expect me to?"

"You didn't want to do this, remember?"

"No, I just didn't think it was a good idea. But I'm having second thoughts on that."

Arianna tipped her head to look at him. "So you *did* think it was a good idea?"

"I was thinking that doing it again would be the good idea."

She bit down on her bottom lip to keep from smiling, but she was sure it carried in her eyes.

"I think we should eat first," she offered as she brushed her fingertips over the hair on his chest.

John gave a glance at his watch. "Too late for grilling, I think."

Arianna gave a grunt. "I only have the few groceries you bought yesterday."

"And I only have Hungry Man dinners."

She propped herself back up on her elbow. "Tell me you have Salisbury steak."

"All of this getting tangled up and your eyes light up with the thought of a Hungry Man salisbury steak dinner?"

She nodded and rolled from the bed.

"Let's go."

"Don't you think you should get dressed first?"

"It's not like we have to drive there."

John shook his head. "And how many times have one of your siblings just showed up?"

She thought about it. Logically, Curtis and Regan were much too busy to just drop by, but then again, she hadn't talked to Carlos in a day which meant he just might check up on her even at, she glanced down at John's watch, eight forty-five.

Arianna crawled back up on the bed and pressed herself up against John. "Maybe we should stay right here for just a little bit longer. You know, at least my clothes are close."

"Thought you were hungry." He brushed his fingers through her hair.

"I think I could wait a little longer. Couldn't you?"

"Oh, hell yeah."

He rolled her onto her back and began what would be another hour of thrilling her and causing her mind to go blank.

Arianna sat at John's kitchen table and watched as he prepared her dinner in the microwave. She felt bad that her house hadn't been put together, but she had to admit that rolling around on the mattress that tried to kill her was much more fun. But now what would happen?

John was quiet again. That was normal, but it was killing her. They had just had mind blowing sex and he wasn't talking. Did he regret it? She sure didn't. She'd like to think they'd do it again and again. This man had occupied her mind for almost a year. She didn't care that he thought he was old. She didn't care about his ex-wife or his crazy work hours. But she was finding she cared an awful lot about him.

The beeping of the microwave snapped her out of her daze, and she looked up to see John remove the dinners and set them on the counter.

"Did you want another beer? I also have soda."

"I just want some water. Where are the glasses?"

He pointed to the cupboard, and Arianna stood to get the glass. There were two.

She glanced at John who was still fussing with the dinners. This man was an island. Two glasses, two coffee cups, a basement apartment with one chair and a tiny couch. People like this didn't invite others into their lives. What had she done?

"You okay?" John touched her arm, and she jumped.

"Fine."

He moved in closer to her and rested his hands on her hips. "You're not feeling bad about what we did upstairs, are you?"

"God, no."

"Good."

She cleared her throat. "Are you?"

John shook his head and raised his hand to her cheek. His warm, rough hand on her skin sent a surge through her that nearly made her knees give out.

He bent slightly and gently brushed her lips with his. "I'm not going to lie. I'm still not sure this is the right thing, but I'd say we are two, very mature individuals. We will handle it."

That stopped the warmth that had coursed through her veins. "Handle it? What's to handle. We kissed. We had sex. Great, amazing sex."

"And you are Regan's sister, and Zach is my boss. I watched him grow up. Now I'm sleeping with you and…"

"Had sex with me," she snapped out. "You're not sleeping with me."

He pulled her in tighter. "So I can't convince you to stay down here tonight? My heat works really well, my bed is made, and my coffeemaker is plugged in."

Arianna dropped her shoulders. "John, what are we doing?"

He kissed her again. "It looks like we're letting our dinner get cold."

"I didn't come back to get into a relationship. I…" She stopped and gathered her thoughts. "I don't want you to hate me."

"I don't think that is possible."

"And you still want to spend time with me? You don't think we made a mistake?"

"Oh, I think it was a big mistake, but honey, I'd been thinking about it for a long time."

"Okay, before this goes any further, we have an agreement. If this having sex in the same house we both live in doesn't work out, we can't be awkward around each other. I mean, you can't go quitting your job over it or never being part of my sister's life. I can't be responsible for you not being around the people who are family to you too. Does that make sense?"

"It means we have to act like grownups?"

"Right," the words squeaked out of her throat.

"So, asking you to be my girlfriend would be childish?"

He was grinning at her, and she was standing there wondering what was wrong with this man. "Girlfriend? I just told you I didn't come home to get involved with someone."

"Well, I don't sleep around." He let his hand drop, and then he walked back to their dinners. "I expect that if a woman is sleeping with me, she's not sleeping elsewhere."

"Are you a possessive man?"

"Over the women I care about, I am." He hadn't had to think about that.

"So, what do you want out of this?"

He picked up the trays and held them in his hands. "I want to enjoy my time with you as I always have. It just happens that I didn't do so well keeping my hands off of you. I'd like to think if we're going to be having sex that we'd have some kind of agreement to have sex with each other and not just when one of us isn't busy with someone else. I'd like to think you'll eat your cold dinner and climb into bed with me. Maybe we could have a little more of what we had upstairs before we fall asleep. Tomorrow I'd like to wake with you in my arms, have a cup of coffee, read the paper on my day off, and watch a playoff game. But I'd like you to be here for it."

He walked to the table and set down their dinners. "That's what I want, Arianna. I'm not going to ask you to marry me. I'm not even going to ask you to stay more than this one time. I'm too old to start over, but I'd sure like to make my time worthwhile. And, since I haven't stopped thinking about you since Carlos's wedding, I figure you must mean something to me."

He pulled out a chair and motioned to it as if he wanted her to sit.

She did so, with the empty glass still in her hand.

"Honey, that's all I got."

She wasn't sure she'd ever heard the man talk that much ever.

Now she was speechless. She nodded her head and sat down.

They ate in silence, and with John, that was comfortable.

And the more that she wanted to hate the fact that she'd crossed the line that she'd hope she wouldn't cross because now things were a bit awkward, she couldn't help but want to say she was his girlfriend. Was it completely crazy to think that perhaps she'd already fallen in love with him?

CHAPTER SEVEN

Monday mornings didn't bother John, but this one had him itchy.

He didn't want to be on edge. After all, he'd spent a great deal of Sunday lounging in his recliner with Arianna either on his lap or very nearby. They'd made love multiple times and eaten the last of his Hungry Man meals. The only thing that should have been making him so antsy was that he'd had to leave.

But now he had to face Zach.

John paced in front of Mary Ellen's desk. He was too early. It wasn't as if he couldn't open the door and wait on Zach's couch. He did own a key to Zach's elevator, but it wasn't right. The whole thing wasn't right.

Production meetings on Monday mornings were supposed to be about the build, not about how he'd *produced* with Zach's sister-in-law. To make matters worse, he was about to ask Zach for something that meant commitment—all for a woman.

He loosened the button on his shirt. The air seemed to be restricted from his head.

Zach's office door opened from the inside, and Mary Ellen stepped out.

"John, you're early." She smiled as she sat down at her desk. "You can go in. He'd never mind having you early."

"Is he in a good mood?"

"A little sleep deprived, but that's to be expected."

John nodded. "He should have taken more time off."

Mary Ellen shook her head and opened the file on her desk. "Right. And when was the last time you took off?"

He couldn't even remember, but suddenly taking a day, or even a week, off to hold Arianna in his arms on some secluded beach sounded more appealing than working. That told him he was in trouble. He loved his job. No woman had ever taken his mind off of it.

John stepped into Zach's office and shut the door behind him. It was bad enough he was nervous. He didn't need Mary Ellen hearing what he'd come for.

Zach was on the phone. When he saw John, he looked down at his watch and then back up at him. Yeah, he'd thrown everyone for a loop by being two hours early.

He sat down on the couch until Zach finished his phone conversation and then stood when Zach hung up.

"You're early."

"So I was told."

"Everything okay? You don't even have your files."

John looked down at his empty hands and realized he'd had no intentions of bringing them. Dear God, he was losing his mind over a woman.

"I'll come back for the meeting later." He stood from the couch and walked toward Zach's desk. "I had something else to talk to you about."

"Sit down. What's up?"

John took a seat. He wasn't comfortable. This was what sleeping with Arianna had done to him. Now he wasn't comfortable in Zach's presence.

"Rockwell Theater."

"Slated for demolition for an office building."

John nodded. "But it's still for sale. The owner wants someone to renovate it. He doesn't want to sell so he hasn't committed yet."

"You know an awful lot about this." Zach leaned back in his chair and crossed his arms over his chest.

"Arianna mentioned something about moving home and having a community theater. She'd like to teach or something like that."

"And you're thinking it would be a good place for her?"

"It was a thought."

Zach moved in and rested his arms on his desk and clasped his hands together. It was a move John was familiar with. It meant he was thinking business.

"Can she afford property like that?"

John shrugged. "I don't know. I haven't even told her about it. I thought you should look at it. I'd be willing to invest in it and see what she could do with it."

"You'd invest?"

"I live in a basement and drive a truck with two hundred thousand miles on it. I have some money stashed away."

The business look changed and the corners of Zach's lips curled into a tight smile. "You'd do this for her."

"It's an investment."

"It sure is."

John stood up. "Listen, if you think it's a bad idea…"

"No." Zach stood and walked around the desk. "I think it's a wonderful idea. I just want to make sure that you're sure about this."

"Investment."

"And you're sure?"

No, he wasn't sure. His chest hurt, his palms were sweaty, and he felt as though Zach had socked him in the gut. But he was crazy about the woman who had made it very clear that marriage was not an option. However, maybe an investment in her livelihood was.

"I think it would be an awesome opportunity for some renovating the area. She'd do the rest."

Zach nodded slowly. "I'll look into it."

"Thanks. I'll be back with my files."

"How about I pick you up at lunch, and we'll head out to Steve's. Since you mentioned it, I've had a hankering for it."

"Sure." John walked out of the office.

For a man who didn't like commitment, he'd sure made one, and now Regan would start asking questions—that part he was sure about.

Arianna had successfully found the coffeemaker. Why she'd packed it with the bathroom items she wasn't sure, except those were all of the last items she'd packed.

The house was beginning to look more like a home.

She'd gone to the store and bought groceries. There was, in fact, a Starbucks at the end of the street so she stopped. And because she couldn't help herself, she picked up some of that imported beer John drank.

Now she looked around and thought how barren it all was. She'd felt more at home in John's basement earlier when she'd gone through the door, which they'd left unlocked, and placed the beer and replacement Hungry Man dinners in his refrigerator.

It wasn't something she needed to get worked up over. She'd given him her word that she wasn't one to sleep around either, and she wasn't. They'd kidded that they were boyfriend and girlfriend. She'd been very candid about never wanting to be married or have babies. But as she sat down on her own couch and turned on her own TV, she missed him.

New relationships were the hardest, and she'd had her share. When they started, you missed the person. You wanted to sleep at their place always. Phone calls and text messages could get you through the day, but it was never enough. Then there was the need to move in together and talk about futures. That was when it usually went wrong.

So where did they go now? They already lived together. Neither of them wanted marriage. Was this all there was to them?

She rested her head back against the couch.

She needed her sister. Regan would know what to do. It had only been two days, and she knew she was about to spill it all. All she could hope was that John wouldn't be upset.

Arianna sat on Regan's couch and held Spencer as he slept. One thing was for sure, the Kellers made beautiful babies.

She'd played with Tyler after lunch until Regan had put him down for a nap. Now the house seemed quiet. She wondered how her mother ever managed with four kids who were all within four years in age.

Regan strolled back into the living room and sat down on the opposite end of the couch. "I think he already likes you."

"What's not to like? I'm here to spoil them rotten."

"Yes, you do that well."

Spencer stretched in her arms. "Thanks for letting me come out."

"Are you kidding me? I'm so happy you're here for good. That once every few months thing was okay, but I'm glad to have my sister back in town."

"I will try not to intrude."

"As you can see, my daily conversations need some adult interaction."

Arianna nodded. "I just couldn't sit in that house anymore. I'm all unpacked, but it was too quiet. New York is never quiet."

"And I'm sure your tenant doesn't make much noise either."

There was a heaviness in her heart when she thought about it. She hadn't even heard him get ready and leave for work that morning. She'd awaken in his bed, alone.

"He's the quiet type."

"Yes, but other than Zach, I've never met a better man."

Arianna ran her thumb over Spencer's tiny hand. "He's been very helpful with the house."

"I've heard he's fed you a few times too."

She laughed. "Yes. I can't seem to buy him a meal. But I did get him some groceries when I went to the store, to pay back some groceries he shared." That was as far as she wanted to go with her admission.

"I hope you don't mind me saying this, but I think he has eyes for you."

"What makes you say that?"

"Because he nearly drove over Carlos to pick you up at the airport the other day. He's talked about you for months, asking how you were, and what you were doing next."

"He did?" Her voice creaked. She'd had no idea.

"Sure." Regan shrugged as if it were no big deal. "I think he's had eyes on you since Zach's father passed away, but he's not one to make a move."

Arianna adjusted the baby on her lap, more out of nervous energy than necessity. "He's mentioned he's not the type to remarry."

"Nah, but just think of how perfect that would be for you. You never want to get married either."

"Still, a relationship is a relationship."

"Yes, and you're not against relationships. You're against the whole issue that there is a document that says you belong to someone else."

Her sister knew her so well.

"What would you say if I told you I was interested in him?"

Regan shifted and leaned in closer. "I'd say you have good taste. He's a very handsome man."

That he was. "What if I told you I kissed him?"

Regan lifted an eyebrow. "I'd say you're very bold."

"That's no news there."

"No, but I would assume it didn't go too well. John's worried that all women are too young for him."

"He does have an issue with age difference."

Regan scooted closer. "He's only in his early fifties. That's not too old."

And didn't she know that, too? Damn! She'd never been with a man who had more energy, and she certainly wasn't going to complain.

"I like him," Arianna admitted to her sister as much as to herself.

"And he likes you, so what's holding you back?"

"Nothing."

"Nothing as in you're going to make a move or…" She studied Arianna and then scooted closer. "Oh, my, God!"

"Shhh," she warned as Spencer shifted.

"You had sex," she whispered.

"We had sex."

Regan's face was not hiding her emotions. The grin on her face was from ear to ear, and if her son hadn't been sleeping in Arianna's arms, she would surely have grabbed her. Of this, she was certain.

"I can't believe it." Regan sat back against the couch and tucked her feet up under her. "How was it?"

"I didn't come here to discuss details like that."

"Really. Usually you would."

"This is different."

"Different?" She studied her again. "You're in love with him."

Arianna let out a long sigh. "I think I am."

"That's wonderful."

"But we already live in the same house. It's as if we've started a relationship at the end. This can't go well."

"Be a little optimistic."

Regan was right. It wasn't as if he'd offered marriage or any enormous commitment. If all else failed, she'd rent out the house again. Regan had lots of room for the favorite aunt.

Zach had met John for lunch, and in true Zach style, he already had figures on the theater.

The price was much more than John could take on himself, but then again, Arianna wouldn't hear of that anyway. Zach had known that, too. He'd offered up capital from Benson, Benson, and Hart. It was an investment for them all—if she'd see it that way.

John stopped by the store on his way home and picked up two steaks, a couple potatoes, and salad. There was no snow on the porch, so there was no reason not to cook her dinner. He couldn't help himself either as he'd checked out. There was a fresh bouquet of flowers, and he bought them. That might have become too domestic, but the thought that they'd bring her some joy made it worthwhile.

He'd pulled up in back of the house, which was the norm. The house looked dark, all but the one light from her bedroom window.

He climbed out of his truck and headed toward the house with his groceries in his hand. The debate of whether to go in through the back door or straight down to his apartment jostled in his mind.

They were in a committed relationship. They'd agreed on that like school children writing notes that said yes or no on them. So why was he so uncomfortable just walking into the house?

He pushed open the door to his apartment and set the groceries on his kitchen table. The door which led to her kitchen was open. That alone was invitation enough, wasn't it?

Maybe he needed his nightly beer to put things into perspective. His routine was just disrupted. He needed one regular moment to make it all fall into place.

John opened the door to the refrigerator and was more than surprised to find it stocked with beer.

Out of sheer curiosity, he opened the freezer and his meals had been replaced, too.

The thought that he should be happy seemed to be clouded by the thought that maybe she was replacing what she felt she owed him. He'd fed her and supplied the beer. He was really going to be pissed if she bought him a new can of coffee.

When he opened that cupboard only his can remained.

It was silly, right? He'd bought her flowers and dinner. Why should he think she didn't want him after the weekend they'd shared?

He knew why, because after years of marriage, his own wife hadn't wanted him. Arianna was thirteen years his junior. At some point, she was going to want a man who wasn't gray or watching his cholesterol.

The unmistakable sound of Arianna walking down the stairs filled his ears. Then the sound of her walking through the kitchen had his heart beat ramping up.

It was time to face the music. Worst case scenario, he'd order a pay-per-view movie and drink his beer.

John gathered his groceries, two of the beers, and the bouquet of flowers and headed up the stairs. As he reached the top, her cell phone rang. He slowed.

She answered the call and repeated "Hello" over and over before grunting.

John turned the corner and Arianna jumped, obviously startled by his presence.

"You scared the hell out of me. I guess we need a bell for your neck."

This was going to be rather interesting, he decided. A new woman—a new bad mood to learn.

"I'm sorry. I thought I'd cook you dinner."

Her shoulders dropped and her eyes softened. "Thank you. I'd really appreciate that."

"I bought you some flowers too, although they are stuck in my hand. Can you grab them?"

He laughed easily and she loved that—liked that. His mind was scrambled.

She took the bag of groceries from around his fingers and the flowers from his hand.

"This was extremely thoughtful of you."

He swallowed hard. "I thought you'd enjoy them."

"You were right."

She set them on the table with the groceries and turned back to him. She took the beers from his hands and set them on the table, too.

Arianna moved back to him and wrapped her arms around his neck. "Before you start getting all domestic on me, I want to kiss you."

"You definitely made my purchase worthwhile."

Her lips were warm as they pressed against his. His hands came to her hips, and he pulled her closer to him. The way her body molded right to his made him wonder, if two people seemed so right for each other, why had it taken so damn long for them to find one another?

As Arianna pulled back, she let out a deep long sigh and then opened her eyes.

"I've waited all day for that."

John was glad to hear that. Why had he even worried? "So who called?"

"What?"

"When I was walking up the stairs. Actually..." He began to realize it wasn't his business at all. "You don't have to tell me."

"No, that's fine. I don't know who it was." She picked up her phone from the table. "It's a blocked number, and it has called me nearly ten times in the last two weeks."

"And no one is there?"

"No."

"And you don't know who it is?"

Her lips turned down. He didn't like that.

Arianna shook her head. "No. I don't know who it is."

But he didn't buy that.

He'd have to not worry about it. She was allowed her secrets. He sure had his.

CHAPTER EIGHT

Arianna set the table, but her hands shook. She'd silenced her phone and stuck it in her pocket. It had rung three more times since John had gone out on the porch to grill steaks.

She could only imagine who it was and that made anger pump through her veins.

That stupid son of a bitch was playing mind games, but why? What could he gain by messing with her?

Regan certainly wouldn't leave her family for him, nor would Arianna ever tell him what she knew about their baby's whereabouts. Regan had never even looked at her baby when she'd had her. She'd forced Curtis to take her away. Besides, that had been four years ago. Why cause problems now?

Arianna looked out the window. She could see John standing on the porch in his heavy coat. His breath carried on the cold. Would he protect her?

Of course he would. He personally knew Alexander Hamilton, and he knew what kind of monster the man was. If he cared for her at all, he'd never let the monster near her or her family.

But that was a lot to ask of the man you were sleeping with.

Then again, she needed to admit. It was more than that.

It wasn't just sex when she had to run and tell her sister about it. It wasn't just physical when the very thought of his smile made her warm. This went deeper.

The flowers he'd brought her were now in a vase on the kitchen table. She couldn't remember the last time a man brought her flowers. Obviously it hadn't mattered. These flowers mattered.

She heard the lid of the grill close, and a moment later, the back door opened and John walked through with cold air blowing in behind him.

"I must have wanted steak really bad. I'm sure my blood is frozen in my veins."

"We could have gone out for steak."

John shook his head as he set the platter down on the table. "No way. I've learned something about you. You spare no expense on things you'll personally use. Your grill is no exception."

She laughed. "Carlos bought the grill when he lived here."

"Okay, so your family has good taste."

She thought about her siblings and their significant others. Yes, her family had good taste, and she must have it, too. John Forrester was a catch, and not one of her family members would disagree.

They ate dinner in silence. It seemed to be the way the man worked. It wasn't until she'd pushed her plate away that John looked up at her to speak.

"You wouldn't want to take a drive, would you?"

Arianna shrugged her shoulders. "If you'd like to."

"I have something I want to show you."

"It's almost eight. You want to show me something in the dark?"

His lips pursed. "Yes."

John wasn't sure she'd take him up on his offer, but he simply couldn't hold out any longer. He drove through Nashville with Arianna seated right next to him. If ever there was a reason to keep a truck with an old bench seat, this was one of them.

George Strait was on the iPod, and the hum of the heater filled any void where silence might become awkward. He knew he was in his own kind of heaven.

Arianna watched the sights of the city, in full swing, from the window. She rested her head on his shoulder. "Are we just going to pass each of these bars or go in one? I mean, at least we're in a city where there is ample entertainment."

"We're almost there."

He saw the building in the distance. Without any of the lights on, it made the entire neighborhood dark. The sight was eerie and unsettling.

John pulled the truck up in front and parked.

Arianna looked around. "This is where you wanted to go?"

"What do you think?"

She looked around and then back at him. "Of what?"

"The building. It's the old Rockwell Theater."

She narrowed her eyebrows as if she were trying to remember something. "The last show they did here was a community version of Phantom, right?"

He chuckled. "I have no idea. I have to admit, theater isn't my thing—usually."

Arianna let out a grunt and then turned her attention back to the building. "So, why are we here?"

"They have the building slated for demolition unless someone buys it and renovates it."

He watched her process the information. "So, it's for sale?"

"Yes."

He couldn't quite read her and that bothered him.

"You'd mentioned that you'd like to do community theater and teach."

"I did." Her words were drawn out slowly.

John turned in his seat to face her. "I have a business proposition for you."

"I'm listening." Again, her words stretched out.

"I've worked for Benson, Benson, and Hart since I was twenty. I learned a trade under Zach's grandfather and was promoted under Zach's father. I took Zach to work with me for years, teaching him a trade. They've always taken care of me." He was rambling. "Point is, other than my TV, my recliner, and my import beer, I've never needed for anything—until now."

He heard her suck in a breath. "What does that mean?"

"It means I would like to buy this theater, with some matched investment capital from Benson, Benson, and Hart."

She nodded. "And what are you going to do with that?"

"That's my business offer for you. I want to help you renovate it and open your theater."

"You want to buy me a theater?"

"Well, no. Yes. What I mean is it's an investment. I know you can do this, and I want to help."

This time she crossed her arms, and he knew that wasn't a good sign. She contemplated for a moment longer. "I don't know what I want to do."

"You told me…"

"I know what I told you. I didn't think you were listening."

If she'd only known what he'd been hearing for the past year. "If this isn't what you want…"

"I don't want to owe anyone."

"It wouldn't be like that."

"It would be exactly like that. I'd owe you and Zach."

"But you'd have this." He raised his hands as if to present the theater.

She sat there silent for a moment longer. "I'm cold. I think I'd like to go home."

John let out a deep breath and headed back home. He'd really taken a chance on her needs, and he'd failed miserably. That was it. He was bad with women, and this one was no different. He'd thought he'd known what his wife had wanted too, but obviously he hadn't delivered.

He was surprised she wasn't allergic to the flowers he'd brought her. That would have been the frosting on the cake.

Just as they pulled up behind her house, her phone rang. She pulled it from her pocket and silenced it.

"Same caller?" he asked.

"I'd assume so."

He turned off the engine and turned to look at her. "Is there something I should know?"

"Such as?"

"Why did you move home?"

"My family is here."

"Why now?"

"I missed everyone. Isn't that enough? And with Spencer and Avery now, I think this is where I belong."

He didn't doubt that was some of the truth. "But you were on Broadway, and amazing I might add."

She chuckled. "You are one loyal employee to have come to New York with Zach and Regan to see me perform."

John let out a grunt and climbed out of the truck. By the time he'd skirted the hood, she was out of the truck and slamming her door.

"Is that why you think I went to New York? Because Zach asked me to?"

Her eyes opened wide as his voice rose.

"Did it ever occur to you that I came because I was interested? I wanted to see you?"

Now her mouth had opened, but she seemed to have a lack of words, so he continued.

"I want that theater for you because I thought you wanted it—to write and teach and perform, not because I need a pet project and not because Zach needs another investment." He stepped up closer to her, and his breath carried in the cold air. "This is a commitment, or at least as close as I can get to one. Don't you see that? The reason I went to Carlos's weddings with you was because, when you showed up to help with Tyler Benson's funeral four years ago, you turned my head. I went to New York because you interested me. I was your date because you fascinated me. Now I have the honor of holding you at night, and I'm beside myself. Hiding and holding back isn't helping the situation. You're keeping secrets from me and that makes me leery of my feelings for you. If you can't tell me who the caller is, how can I trust that you'll keep your promise to me to be exclusively mine?"

She gasped at that.

John wanted to pull her into his arms and hold her, but he was mad. "Don't be so strong-willed that you won't let the man who loves you take care of you or do something for you. You never know when they will grow tired of trying."

And with that he walked away because he'd said more than he'd meant to.

Cold air closed in around Arianna as she watched John walk down the outside steps to his apartment. When the door slammed, she knew she'd acted childish.

But how was she supposed to react? It was dark, and he was showing her buildings with grand plans for her to make something big of it. That scared the hell out of her, but not nearly as much as him saying something about loving her.

Her phone buzzed in her pocket again. She pulled it out, but this time it was a text message. *You'll fail!*

As she read it, a picture came through as well. It was her and John in his truck outside the Rockwell Theater.

Arianna swallowed hard. He was following her.

She looked around the alley and her yard. He could be anywhere. She wasn't safe standing in her own backyard with John only feet away. And if she wasn't safe, neither was Regan.

It was time to come clean. She had to tell John about Alexander Hamilton. Something had to be done.

Arianna ran to the house and up the back stairs. She shook as she pushed her key into the lock and turned it. But when she heard the inside door to John's apartment close and the deadbolt from his side lock, she knew he wasn't going to listen now.

She bolted the back door, ran up to her bedroom, and locked the door. Tomorrow she would tell Carlos. She didn't want to worry Regan or Curtis with it yet. Maybe they could head him off.

CHAPTER NINE

It had been one of the longest nights in Arianna's life. She'd heard the shower at four that morning, and John drove away by five. Obviously he was still mad.

She'd make it up to him. She didn't want him to hate her. They did have a commitment. He was right. There was no reason to ruin it over her reaction to something so thoughtful.

Sunshine had finally made it through the drapes. It was time to face the day and her feelings.

After her shower she brewed a pot of coffee, but it went cold before she'd poured the first cup. Her mind wasn't on the normal activity of the day. It was on that stupid building John wanted to buy.

But it wasn't stupid.

Arianna sat at the kitchen table and held her head in her hands. It was a wonderful building. She'd seen *Annie* there when she was five. That was what had given her the acting bug. There was a history with her and that theater, so why had she freaked out?

Perhaps her community theater group could do *Annie* there. Clara would make an amazing Annie.

Her mind was brewing now, so she started another pot of coffee and searched through a box she'd thrown in the hall closet for a notebook and a pen.

By noon she'd had two pots of coffee, no food, and had the notebook nearly full of ideas. There were voice lessons to be had and method acting classes to teach. She had a list of four different productions that would be great to get the kids in the community involved in. Maybe one night they'd have an open mic night, and with the number of music industry leaders in the community, perhaps someone would get their break on her stage.

The ideas just kept coming.

By two in the afternoon, she finally changed out of her robe, tied her hair in a tail on the top of her head, and headed into town to look at the building herself.

The view in broad daylight wasn't much different than the view she'd had the night before. It was worn down and unloved.

Arianna stepped out of her car and looked around the street. People bustled around, and she didn't feel as though she was being watched.

She bundled up her coat, locked the car, and crossed the street.

"Your sister knows you better than I thought she did," Zach's voice called from behind her.

Arianna spun to find him walking toward her. "What are you doing here?"

"Regan figured you'd come to look at it yourself. When I called your house and you weren't there, I figured you'd be here."

She let out a deep breath. "John wants to buy this."

"It sold yesterday."

Sadness bolted through her, and she shivered. "Oh. That's too bad."

"New owner wants to make it a community theater or something like that."

She thought about the notebook she'd filled with ideas. It had been a waste of time.

Whoever had sent her the texts last night had told her she'd fail. Perhaps she had.

"Well, no need to stand here staring at it then," she said as she shoved her bare hands into her pockets. "Maybe I'll head out to your house and visit my boys."

Zach pulled a key out of his pocket and handed it to her. "Let's go in and look around first."

She looked at the key and then at him. "What's going on?"

"Benson, Benson, and Hart has a new property. It's going to need some upkeep so I'm going to send my best foreman to oversee the job. Then it's going to need someone to bring it to life. Now, I have this niece who can belt out show tunes, and I've heard my sister-in-law might have done some theater. Maybe I can find her and…"

He didn't finish once she'd charged him and wrapped her arms around his neck. "I won't let you down."

"I know." He kissed her on the cheek. "Let's go inside. And then I'll tell you just how many people have invested in this building."

He started for the stairs, but his comment hung with her. She wasn't sure he had to tell her. There was no doubt her sister was in on it and her parents, too. The Keller family worked fast. But there was probably a hefty investment from John as well. She owed him an apology.

Arianna followed Zach up the front steps. The door creaked as he pushed it open.

The air was stale, and the lobby was nearly pitch black.

"My father taught me well. Always carry a flashlight to a new building," Zach said as he pulled a flashlight from his coat pocket. "I made sure the utilities were on. We just have to find the switch."

She followed close behind him. "How did you get the building so fast?"

"I have some leverage in this town."

"I don't doubt that, but…"

"Just accept it. Okay, here's a switch." He flipped it and rows of lights in the lobby flickered on. "Wow."

Arianna let out a sigh. "Yeah, wow."

The theater had been abandoned longer than they had thought. The lobby had been vandalized. She wasn't so sure of his investment now, and by the look on his face, neither was he.

"Let's see what the auditorium looks like." He reached for her hand and she took it.

Slowly they walked through the heavy doors into the theater.

She was sure the lights were in the back, but she didn't need lights to see what a mess it was.

Chairs were ripped from the floor, sconces on the wall hung by wires, and the stage was covered in junk.

"I think John's vision for this place was off," she said with a hitch in her voice.

"I don't think so. He wouldn't have mentioned it to me if he didn't think it would work."

"He thinks he can make this place look nice?"

Zach turned to her, but even in the dark, she could see the glimmer in his eyes. "He knows he can. You don't underestimate him, do you?"

She shook her head. No, she certainly didn't.

"I think we're going to need more light before we even try to go deeper into this building. Let's say we head back to my office and make some plans.

"That sounds good. Would I mess you up completely if I made a stop first?"

She saw the smile that formed on his lips. It was all out in the open now. Regan had spilled the beans—she was toast.

Zach had given Arianna his hard hat from his car. She'd put it on the moment she parked in the lot at the build and climbed out of her car. Zach had told her John would be in the trailer.

She'd never been on a construction site. She looked around, taking in the sights and sounds of where John spent his days. No wonder he was a quiet man. His days were filled with noise.

Carefully she walked up the metal steps to the trailer and pulled open the door.

Almost immediately she heard John yell from beyond the wall, "Shut the damn door. It's freezing."

Arianna clasped her hands together and walked through to where she'd heard his voice. "It is freezing. Do you have coffee in this place?"

John had been looking at blue prints, but when she'd spoke his head snapped up. At first there was a smile in his eyes, but a moment later it was gone.

"What are you doing here?"

"I came to see you."

"Zach sent you?" He motioned to her hat.

She pulled it from her head. "Oh, he let me borrow this." She hadn't realized his name was on it.

"I'm really busy right now. Maybe I can talk to you at home."

Arianna didn't like this side of John, but the worst part was she knew she'd created it.

"I want to talk now."

John flattened his hands on the table then stood up straight and crossed his arms over his chest.

She gripped tightly to the helmet. "I was childish last night. I'm sorry."

"Doesn't matter."

"But it does." She took another step closer. "I know you invested in the building."

"You're not supposed to know that."

"Okay, I didn't know that for a fact until just this moment, but thank you."

He shook his head and rolled his eyes. She'd caught him on that fact, and he wasn't any happier about it.

"This morning I made a lot of plans for that building before I knew it was really mine to make plans for. But the point is, you were thinking of me."

"That's been my problem lately. That's all I think about."

Finally the chill that ached in her muscles eased. "You're all I've been thinking about, too."

She walked around the table that separated them and stood next to him.

"You said something else last night. Something about taking care of the woman you loved."

He nodded slowly. "I didn't think you were listening."

"I heard you. And a woman wouldn't hide anything from the man she loved." His eyes flickered for a moment when she said it, but he stayed quiet.

Arianna pulled her phone from her pocket and pulled up the text message. "This came through last night."

He took the phone from her and looked at the text message and picture. "Son of a bitch!"

"It has to be the same blocked phone from the calls."

"If I find this guy…"

"It's Alexander Hamilton."

If a man's blood could actually boil, John's was close.

"How the hell do you know that?"

Arianna's shoulders dropped. "That's why I moved back here so quickly. He came to me in New York and wanted to know where Regan's baby was."

"The baby she gave up?"

Arianna nodded. "He's crazy. The man doesn't want Regan or that child. He wants to hurt her."

He knew that well enough. He'd seen him take after her in L.A., and then he'd seen Zach take in after Alexander. He shouldn't have pulled Zach off of him. Perhaps he should have let him kill the bastard.

"He's stalking you?"

"I don't know if this is him, but I assume it has to be."

"We need to go to the police."

She touched his arm. "I'm not worried about me, but we need to protect Regan."

John left his work on the table, grabbed Arianna by the arm, and led her straight to his truck.

Two hours later they had filed a report, but there was nothing the police could do and that had him angrier than before.

He sat at the stoplight on the way back to the site, gripping his steering wheel. He hadn't even noticed he hadn't spoken until Arianna reached across the cab and touched his leg.

"You're very quiet," she said softly.

"I'm pissed off."

"I know, but you heard them. There is no proof it's him, and they can't do anything about it."

"No, but we can be on the lookout. That bastard is crazy, and I'm not about to let him touch you like he touched your sister. And he's not getting his hands on her or that child either."

He heard what he thought was a sob, so he took his eyes off the road and saw Arianna gazing at him.

"What's wrong?"

"Not a thing. I've never felt so safe."

"Well, I wish you would have told me about this before you even moved back. What if he'd gotten to you again? What if…"

"I love you."

He gripped the steering wheel tighter. "You love me because I've made you feel safe?"

"No, I'm very certain I've loved you for a long time. The feeling safe, that's just a bonus."

He nodded. He'd started this last night by telling her he'd care for the woman he loved, and of course, he'd meant her. But was she expecting him to say those words to her? Did she need validation?

When he stopped at the next light and looked over at her, she was smiling and watching the people move about the city from her window. He needed to tell her, but not under these circumstances. She needed to know it was a sentiment from his heart, not out of need.

"I think we need to get everyone together and tell them what is going on," he said as he eased off the brake and shifted the truck into gear.

"I think we should have everyone meet at Mom and Dad's."

"Start calling. We can't wait. We need to do it now."

By seven o'clock, the entire Keller family was assembled around Arianna's parents' dining room table.

The room had grown smaller over the years with spouses and children.

Usually the room bustled with noise and laughter, but the atmosphere was different now. They'd all joined there because Arianna had asked them to, but they knew something was wrong. And how she was going to ease into it, she wasn't sure.

"John and I needed to share something with all of you."

Regan lifted Spencer to her shoulder and narrowed her eyes on Arianna. "The funny part about all this is I'd like you to follow up that sentence with something like *we're getting married.* But with your tone and the look on your face, if you tell me you're dying I'm going to lose it."

"I'm not dying."

"Good," Madeline spoke up. "I've already tried that. Let's leave that subject alone."

Carlos put his arm around his wife's shoulders and gave her a squeeze. "So why are we all here?" he asked.

Arianna let out a long, slow breath as John took her hand in his and interlaced his fingers with hers. He knew she couldn't tell them and keep them calm. She gave him a nod.

John acknowledged and looked at her family. "The reason Arianna moved back to Nashville was because she had a visit from Alexander Hamilton in New York."

Zach was the first to come out of his seat, followed by Curtis.

The vein in Zach's neck bulged, and his face turned red. "That maniac came to you, and you didn't tell anyone? He's on American soil, and I haven't killed him?"

Regan placed her hand on his arm. "You're going to scare Tyler."

"Regan, if he even steps foot in this state..."

"I think he has," Arianna interrupted.

Curtis was swift as he came around the table and turned her toward him. "We're not playing games with this. You know what he did to her." He pointed to Regan. "You should have told us what was going on."

Tears rolled down her cheeks, and she couldn't stop the sobs that had taken over her breathing. She was the one always in control, and now she didn't know what to do as that control slipped.

"I'm sorry. I'm so sorry."

John pulled her into his arms and held her close. "Listen, the point is he's out there. He's been calling her and hanging up. Last night she got a text message and a picture of us outside the theater. If it's not him, someone is following her and that's just as scary."

Simone lifted her head. "I have not spoken to my father in months, but I will call him and ask if he has spoken to the *idiot!*"

Zach shook his head. "He'd wanted Simone's father to invest in a build. I wouldn't have anything to do with it."

"Well, the fact is he's surfacing," John continued to hold her.

Arianna took in a deep breath and tried to calm her nerves. She turned back to her family. "I'm sorry I didn't tell everyone why I came home. John and I have gone to the police and given them the information. There is nothing they can do. They don't have a way of tracking the calls or texts. The phone number doesn't come up."

Arianna's father sat back in his chair and crossed his arms over his chest. "We will protect each other. That is how this family works." He then leaned in on his elbows and took the time to connect with each and every one of them with a glance. "We will do all that is necessary."

That was all that needed to be said.

Strangely enough, Arianna felt more secure than she had in a very long time.

The evening hadn't ended with the bad news about Alexander Hamilton. Once her mother had her family all gathered, she had to cook.

It wasn't anything more than spaghetti and garlic bread, but it was a family meal.

They hadn't spoken about Alexander Hamilton again, but he was on everyone's mind. And if she knew her siblings, they'd all take a shot at her.

As her father moved to the family room with his grandsons Eduardo and Christian close behind, Arianna helped her mother clear the table as her sister and Simone both nursed their babies.

Arianna set the dishes in the sink and opened the dishwasher as her mother walked into the kitchen.

"You're all moved in?"

"Yes. I finally have everything in its place."

"Good. And you're comfortable with John in the basement?"

Arianna began loading the dishwasher. "Yes."

"Ah." Her mother's German accent grew thicker the older she became. Arianna always wondered if it was something that mentally kept her connected to her past. Perhaps if she kept the accent, she'd still have that part of her.

Her mother went about putting away items in the refrigerator as Arianna filled the dishwasher, but then she felt her nearby.

She turned to see her standing with her hands on her hips.

"You don't have anything to share with me?"

"Such as?" Arianna matched her mother's stance.

"You and John. I'm not blind, Arianna. What has happened between the two of you?"

Arianna's hands dropped to her side. "I think I've fallen in love with him. That's what's happened between us."

The swinging door that led into the kitchen opened, and Madeline walked in. "Thank goodness you got that out in the open. I couldn't eavesdrop any longer."

Arianna laughed. Madeline was as close a sister to her as Regan. She'd missed her for years when her brother was so stupid to have divorced her.

"Why did you have to eavesdrop? Regan already knew all of this."

"Of course she did. That's why we all know about it. But I wanted to hear for myself."

Arianna walked to the kitchen table and pulled out a chair. If she and her sister were young, she'd have taken hold of her hair and pulled until she cried for sharing her secrets. Then again, they must not have been very secret if Regan was sharing them. Regan didn't gossip for spite.

By the time she'd sat down, the kitchen filled with Simone and Regan each carrying their babies. Soon Clara was following close behind. Thank goodness she was. At least they wouldn't be embarrassing her about her sex life in front of Clara.

"Clara, are you familiar with the musical *Annie*?" she asked her niece.

"Isn't everyone?"

That was true enough. "You're right. Did you hear that Zach bought a new building, and it's a theater?"

"I thought everyone bought it for *you*," she said innocently as Madeline reached for her and pulled her close.

She gave her an enormous hug from her seat. "No one was supposed to tell her that."

"I didn't know it was a surprise."

Arianna reached for Clara's hand. "It was a wonderful surprise, and I'm going to make you all proud. And I was thinking of *Annie* as the first production. It was the first show I ever saw, and I saw it at the Rockwell Theater."

"That would be neat," Clara said.

"Will you help me with it?"

Clara's eyes widened, and she exchanged glances with Madeline and then looked back at Arianna. "Really?"

"I think you'd be the perfect choice."

"To help you?"

"Yes. But I also thought you'd be a perfect Annie."

CHAPTER TEN

The atmosphere in the truck was much different than on the drive over to Arianna's parents' house. She was at ease, and John wasn't near as tense either.

He'd wrapped his arm around her shoulder once he was on the highway headed home. She rested her head against him.

"I think this theater is going to be wonderful."

He hummed his agreement. "It's going to be a lot of work."

"I know, but I'm ready for that."

"Zach asked me to work on it. He said since it's a Benson, Benson, and Hart acquisition, it's part of my job."

Arianna leaned up against him closer. "So I'll get to see you work?"

"I'm not a nice guy when I work. You might not want to be around."

She lifted her lips to his ear. "You can't get rid of me of me like that. You're stuck with me."

His arm tightened around her shoulders. "That's exactly what I wanted."

By the time they pulled up behind her house, Arianna was completely stirred up. She'd be damned if John slept in his own bed tonight without her. As wound up as she was, he'd be lucky to get any sleep at all.

The moment she opened the back door, she was swept off her feet and thrown over John's shoulder.

She let out a yelp. "What are you doing?" she laughed as he carried her up the stairs like some caveman.

"You ruined my night last night. I seriously don't want to be sleeping alone. So you're going to have to make that up to me."

She was still laughing. "Very aggressive of you."

"I'm a man with a need. And that need is for a shower."

He carried her through the bedroom and to the bathroom where he dropped her on her butt on the vanity.

She sat there while he turned on the shower. When he turned back to her, his eyes were dark. There was, indeed, a fury burning behind them.

Arianna stopped laughing and met his eyes with her own. He turned and reached for her. His hands were tangled in her hair, pulling the band which held her ponytail.

Her hair fell in curls around her shoulders as his mouth took possession of hers.

There was nothing like the fire of a kiss when a man was worked up, but knowing she loved this man, the heat was much greater.

John pressed up against her, and she wrapped her legs around him. His hands were making quick work of her clothes, and she fought with the buttons on his shirt.

Steam from the shower mixed with the pants of hot breath shared between them.

John pulled her from the vanity and shimmied her pants off of her and then quickly undressed himself.

The water was hot, but not as hot as the man who stood before her. He might be sensitive about his age in years, but she'd never seen a man more fit and more sexy than John Forrester.

He pulled her to him and centered them both under the stream of hot water.

His hands slid over her skin, and she held tight to him as her knees grew weak from his touches—his kisses—his passion.

Their love-making in the shower was fast and furious. Soap slicked skin only enhanced each touch—each movement.

John took down the shower head and rinsed them off, his mouth still working against hers.

She had to admit there was stamina with him. There were no robes or towels. There was no time. He helped her from the shower and straight to the bed where he laid her down and quickly moved atop of her—inside her.

Arianna wrapped her arms around him tightly, pulling him closer. Needing him nearer to her than any other person had ever been before.

And when the motions stopped and contentment had been had, she kept him close, his rapid breath strong in her ear.

"I love you, Arianna Keller. I always will."

She fought back the tears which came with his sentiment. There may never be a marriage license or a child bearing their resemblances, but there was the promise of forever. And that was all she'd ever need.

Arianna heard the alarm go off on John's phone the next morning, and it was the first time he'd rolled away from her all night.

He silenced it and wrapped himself around her again.

"Wouldn't your boss be okay with you taking a day off?" she asked with her voice raspy with sleep.

"I don't know. I've never taken a day off."

She grunted. "Never?"

"Never."

She believed that—mostly. If there was a more loyal man than John Forrester, she'd be surprised. And the best part was, if he was that loyal to Zach, she couldn't imagine how loyal he'd be to her.

An hour later he was showered, shaved, dressed, and gone. The house was instantly lonely.

Arianna had her cup of coffee at the kitchen table and looked over her notebook of ideas for the theater. Soon she wouldn't have time to feel alone in her own home—their home.

She put down the notebook. His stuff needed to come upstairs. She wasn't going to marry the man, but she sure as hell wasn't going to let him sleep away from her ever again, even just a few feet away.

Arianna stood up, rinsed out her cup, and got dressed. She wasn't going to move him. That would be the dumbest thing she could ever do. They could leave it as a man cave, but she sure was going to head down to the site with lunch and make him an offer he couldn't refuse.

On her way to the build site, her phone rang. She was seriously going to have to give everyone a special ring tone because just hearing the ring made her antsy.

She looked down in the cup holder where her phone sat. It was Regan.

"Hey, Sis. Did you call to apologize for telling everyone I was sleeping with John?"

Regan laughed on the other end. "Did you think anyone thought you weren't?"

"Pretty transparent, huh?"

"We were at the weddings, too. It was just a matter of time before the two of you ran into each other instead of away from each other."

The comment was true enough. They probably had given everyone some reason to think they'd catch each other in the end. And probably only the two of them didn't know it.

"Are you out and about?" Regan asked.

"Yes, I was headed to the build site to take John some lunch."

"Well, we are all in Zach's office. John is on his way here. Swing by."

"Impromptu meeting?"

"You could say that."

Arianna changed lanes, turned down the nearest street, and headed the opposite direction. "I'm on my way."

She'd only been in Zach's office a few times. She'd thought that if she *had* to work in an office, his was the one she'd want. It was spacious, well decorated, and the view was spectacular.

Zach's assistant escorted her into the office. Zach sat behind his desk with Tyler on his lap, and Regan nursed Spencer on the couch. Just through the other door was Zach's conference room, and she could see John standing over the table with blue prints rolled out and Eduardo stood next to him.

She went directly into the conference room. "Why are you not in school?"

"Apprenticeship. I get school credit for the last two hours of my day if I'm here," Eduardo explained.

"Really? How cool is that?"

John looked up at her. "He's quite an asset, too. He's been working with me for a few months."

There was heaviness in her chest. She didn't even know John spent time with her nephew. Was it that she hadn't heard of the arrangement that bothered her, or that John had never mentioned it?

She tried to push it from her mind. It was petty. She'd been the one that was gone. Why would they ever have called her with news like that?

"So, what are you two studying?" She walked next to John.

It surprised her when he pulled her in next to him and wrapped his arm around her waist. He didn't come across as the kind of man who would show affection in public.

"These are the theater prints."

"Really? You have them already?"

"They're public."

She was certainly new to the whole construction world.

Zach carried Tyler into the room and set him in a chair. "Ed's going to help on the renovation. Is that okay with you?"

"Of course. This is a family theater. All the better if my family is in on it, right?"

"Clara wouldn't shut up about acting last night," Eduardo said. "She was driving me crazy."

"And tonight you'll drive her crazy talking about the blue prints, won't you?"

He chuckled. "Probably."

"What about Christian? Does he have a part in this?"

"I told him he could sell popcorn at intermission."

They all laughed at that.

"Christian doesn't have time for anything other than baseball," Eduardo added.

"We all have our callings." Arianna looked up at John, who looked down at her. And she knew, at that moment, her calling was to be his.

Mary Ellen ordered in Chinese food, and the group spent the next three hours going over plans for the theater. Arianna was pleasantly surprised at how many times John would ask Eduardo's opinion on an item and accept what he had to say.

The electrical would have to be completely redone. All of the seating would need to be replaced. The stage needed to be rebuilt, and of course, the lobby would need to be gutted and redesigned.

"The craziest part about this building is that the curtains are in good condition. They just need to be cleaned," John added.

Zach looked at Arianna. "You'll still want to replace them, I'm sure."

"Oh, I don't know. Wouldn't that be fun to keep? I'll think about it."

Regan left with her boys and Eduardo. Arianna stayed with John and Zach to discuss a time frame for the theater to be ready.

"We're looking at July at the earliest," John said as he tipped back in his seat. "It's almost as though we're starting from scratch."

"We are," Zach commented as he picked up a leftover fortune cookie and broke it open.

Arianna leaned in and rested her arms on the table. "July? That would be enough time to put together something fun for the grand opening, and then, maybe by October, we can have the first, full production ready."

John looked at her with eyes that smiled. "I'm glad to see you get excited over this. You're always beautiful, but talking about this makes you almost sparkle."

She felt the heat rise in her cheeks. "I love what I do."

Zach pushed away from the table. "Arianna, I don't know if I should kiss you for making this fool so happy or send you packing since his head is in the clouds."

"You and Regan set us up, remember?"

"I just didn't think he'd get all soft on me." He stood and walked toward his office. "I'm going home to snuggle on my boys."

"I'll lock up when we leave," John offered.

Zach disappeared into the private elevator in the corner of his office. The building had become quiet.

John stood from his seat and pulled Arianna from hers. His mouth was quickly pressed against hers, and her body settled against his.

He rested his forehead against hers. "I've waited all day to do that."

"You haven't had enough of me yet?"

"The plan is to never have enough of you."

Arianna rested her head against his chest. "So, this is how it will be? You build all day. I'll perform all night?"

John lifted her chin with his finger. "And we will share a bed every night for the rest of our lives."

"The rest of our lives?" She hoped her voice hadn't cracked, but her body shook, so she was sure it had.

"If you'll have me."

"Doesn't this seem sudden?"

He pulled her closer to him. "Honey, we've been working on this, very poorly, for the past four years. I don't ever want to be with anyone else."

"Then, every night for the rest of our lives sounds good to me."

He held her tightly before stepping back and looking at her. "Why were you coming to see me today?"

Warmth filled her knowing they were in love. The moment was perfect. The timing was right. "I'd planned to ask you to move in with me. Upstairs, that is."

"It sounds like we have the same plans."

"Who would have thought it would come together so quickly."

John kissed her again. "You know, Zach has a Murphy bed in the other room."

Arianna slapped his arm. "Let's just get home, quickly."

"To our home?"

"To our home."

John had followed Arianna out to her car and continued to follow her all the way home. She hadn't mentioned that she'd received any more texts or phone calls all day, but he wasn't taking any chances. At least for the next six months, they would be in the same place, and he wondered if that, too, was some of Zach's plan.

Zach had a vested interest in the theater nearly as much as John did. But John knew keeping him near was as good for business as it was for family.

He reached over and turned down the heat in the truck. His body seemed to be plenty warm at the moment, and that was all courtesy of Arianna.

There had been a moment in the conference room where he'd actually contemplated proposing to her, but common sense took over quickly. Neither one of them needed that. They knew what the other wanted. No marriage. No babies. But a commitment was a commitment.

Arianna turned down their street, and he continued to follow. The theater would be their baby. Its conception was in her notebook and in his renovation plans. Its birth would be the grand opening. Its life would be the many lives it could touch.

Their marriage would be their commitment to each other. They'd share a home, a business, and a life.

He watched her park her car in the driveway, and he pulled up behind her.

Her birthday was coming up. He was sure he'd remembered Regan talking about a party for her with Mary Ellen.

She'd need something nice. Just because they weren't going to get married, it didn't mean she couldn't have a really nice ring to wear.

CHAPTER ELEVEN

Renovation started on the theater the following Monday. Arianna was on site with Starbucks in hand by six o'clock.

Zach climbed out of his car and walked toward her. "Just a little excited?"

"You have no idea." She turned to him. "I still can't believe you all did this."

"That's what family is all about."

"You're right. And I'm going to make sure you all get a good return for your investment."

Zach put his arm around her shoulders. "We already have." Arianna shifted to look at him, and he smiled. "You're here with us."

His words squeezed at her heart. "Thank you."

"Regan hasn't been this happy in a long time. Even though she hasn't had a lot of time to spend with you, she's whole now that you're near."

"Oh, I don't know about that. I think you and the boys make her life whole."

"I'd like to think so," he said as he shifted and crossed his arms. "But no matter what, it's always been you two. That makes a difference."

She knew he was right. The Keller family's strength was in its members. And Arianna drew her strength from her brothers and her sister—and now from John.

Arianna remained on the curb even after Zach went inside the theater. There was an amazing feeling which had taken over in her. She'd never understood the connection her sister had to Zach, Carlos to Madeline, or Curtis to Simone. It was nice to watch, but she didn't understand it—until now.

It was going to the extreme for the other person. Zach could have made millions building with Alexander Hamilton, but Regan was more important. Carlos's pride had lost him Madeline once, but even marriage to someone else couldn't keep them apart. Then there was Simone who gave up the life she knew to have an ordinary life with the man she loved.

Arianna had always been content thinking that true love would never happen for her. Thank goodness she'd been wrong.

John walked out the front doors of the theater. "I heard there was a beautiful woman out here just standing on the street."

"And I knew if I stood here long enough, a handsome construction worker would walk out."

He walked down the steps. When he reached her, he kissed her gently on the lips. "You know, it'll be weeks before there is even anything you can do here. No need for you to hang around all day."

"I haven't decided if I want to just be here—to be near it. Or if it's you I want to be near."

He pulled her into his arms. "You make it very hard to get any work done."

Arianna let out a deep sigh. "I suppose Simone could use some company."

"Avery probably needs some spoiling."

"I'm an expert at that."

He kissed her again. "Yes, you are."

Arianna was sure Avery had gained at least five pounds since she'd last held her. And perhaps she had. Simone wasn't as quick to hand over Avery as Regan was with Spencer.

"Will you go back to work at the clinic when Avery is a little older?"

"Does it seem silly that I want to?"

"Why would that seem silly?"

"I never would have thought I, of all people, would want to work. But I enjoy my work. I enjoy helping people."

Arianna smiled. Her future sister-in-law certainly had been humbled.

Simone rocked back on the couch and clasped her hands in her lap. "You do not mind if I ask you a question, do you?"

"Certainly not."

Simone looked down at the ring on her finger, which Curtis had given her, and then back up at Arianna. "You have not had any more phone calls or text messages, have you?"

"Not since the night we all met and discussed it. Why?"

Simone pressed her lips together and then let out a breath. "I made some phone calls. Alexander Hamilton divorced last year. His wife pressed abuse charges against him."

"Bastard."

"She is very well off. Her family is worth billions."

"Which is why he tried to murder Regan." She shook her head. It still hurt to think of what he'd done to her sister.

"Anyway, she left him and he has nothing. His fortune, which he had earned prior to his marriage to her, is gone and now his wife has taken her money."

"And I'm his connection to Regan. What does he want? Revenge?"

"I would assume that is his thought. The man is crazy. I am sure you have met him."

Arianna shook her head. "Only Curtis ever saw the man. I didn't know who he was until he came to the theater in New York." There was more. So much more, but she hadn't even told John about it. She wasn't going to bring it up to Simone.

"He is very dangerous. I hope he just goes away."

So did Arianna.

As hard as John tried, he couldn't keep Arianna away. She was there every morning with her Starbucks for at least an hour to see what was going on.

By two o'clock in the afternoon, John was checking back in on the other build, and by four, he was seated in Zach's office.

"The stage is torn out right now. They should have that put back together in the next week, and the entire interior has been gutted. Time to rebuild," he told Zach.

"Regan says Arianna already has been acquiring some contacts."

"I don't know what she's up to, but she's one busy woman."

Zach nodded. "Regan would like to have Arianna's birthday party at the theater. A surprise party, if we can manage it."

"You think Regan can keep a secret from Arianna?"

Zach laughed. "She wants to try."

John closed his notebook with all of his lists and clasped his hands atop it. "When is the birthday exactly?"

"Four weeks."

"Stage will be done, but the theater isn't going to look pretty."

"She knows, but have you ever tried to reason with Regan."

This time John laughed. Yes he had, and there was no reason to even try to change her mind. "I'll make sure the facilities are in order for guests to use and the stage is done so that we can set up tables and chairs. The theater seats go in last. That's not a problem, is it?"

"No. Just the stage. That's where Regan wants to entertain."

"And your mother is on catering duty."

"She only uses the best ones."

Audrey did have fine taste in everything, John thought.

Zach leaned back in his chair. "What are you going to get her? This is the big one, you know. The big four-oh."

"She hasn't mentioned that. It must not be as big for her as you think."

"That's because she's content. Most women her age either are longing for marriage and babies or watching their children grow into adults. Arianna is happy."

That part John knew.

Zach sat back up in his chair. "Madeline will handle forty just fine. She's been through enough to appreciate it and her kids are amazing. Regan, well, I won't even speculate. Now Simone…"

John shook his head. "You are the only man alive that could get away with that thought you're having."

"Yep. I don't even think Curtis would try."

"How are they doing?"

"I've never seen Simone happier in my life. Who would have thought a woman would fall into my lap, and I'd marry her. And not only that, she'd come with a brother for my best friend and a sister for my right-hand man."

John drove home in afternoon traffic, and Luke Bryan played on his iPod, which was situated next to him as the radio had stopped working years ago. As soon as Taylor Swift started singing about never, ever, ever, ever getting back together, he turned it off. This was what happened when you fell in love with a younger woman. She filled your iPod with songs from men she'd mentioned, who wore their jeans nice and tight, and girls who weren't old enough to know about the love they sang about.

He'd need to make sure, if he was going to let her access his music, she'd better keep some Johnny Cash and Hank in there. He might just go crazy if she switched it all out.

When he finally made it home and walked through the back door, he laughed when she had the stereo blasting and this time is was Patsy Cline. Well, she was a mystery, this young woman he loved.

He walked into the living room and found the volume control and turned it down.

"Hey!" he heard yelled from upstairs.

"I figured that would get your attention." He pulled off his coat and draped it over his arm. Suddenly he'd become very aware of the fact he'd walked into the house with his work boots on. Just as quickly as he'd walked in, he retreated to the back door to pull them off.

Arianna skipped down the steps and out to the kitchen. "Guess what?"

"What?"

"I just secured *Annie* for the grand opening in October."

The smile on her face was infections, and he felt his cheeks rise as he smiled, too. "That's wonderful."

"I've already called my brother and asked him if it would be okay if I offered the part to Clara."

John hung his coat on the hook by the door. "You're not going to audition her?"

"Perks of knowing the director. Besides, have you ever heard the girl sing?"

He shook his head.

"You'll understand when you hear her. She's going to be a star someday. Just you wait."

John wondered if she was that excited about her nieces and nephews, how excited would she be over the talents of her own children. Would she have them on stage singing and dancing? Would he have them with hammers and nails?

His jaw tightened. Where had that come from?

He could feel the blood drain from his head.

"Are you okay?" Arianna was moving to him quickly. "You're pale."

"I'm fine." He batted her away and brought his mind back to the conversation about *Annie* and Clara. "Do you think Clara will want to work that hard?"

Arianna's eyes were narrowed on him, but once he moved through the kitchen and pulled a beer from the refrigerator, she loosened up. "Yes. We are so much alike, her and I. She'll be very excited. In fact, I'm going to head over there now. I was digging this up from a box upstairs."

She held up a CD case with the music from *Annie*.

John nodded. "Mind if I go with you? We could pick up some dinner."

"I would adore that." She moved into him and pressed a kiss against his lips.

He was sure she'd meant to leave it at that, but he needed more.

John wrapped his arms around her waist and pulled her in closer. He moved his mouth over hers and took the kiss deep, to another level.

Arianna's arms came up around his neck. Oh, what this woman could do to him with just one kiss.

She pulled back, but kept him close. "We'd better go or I'll never make it over there."

At least he knew his kisses did the same to her. He wondered how quickly they could eat and offer a position to Clara. He had some needs brewing, and by the blush on her cheeks, she did too.

CHAPTER TWELVE

One thing John had forgotten about was in-laws. Sure, Carlos and Madeline weren't his, but if he'd planned a life with Arianna, and he did, then he'd suppose this was the way of it.

He certainly didn't mind Carlos. Heck, if he had to have a brother-in-law, he'd have chosen him personally. He'd never seen a harder working man. But the part he'd forgotten about was when you "stopped by," you couldn't leave.

Carlos and Christian had just returned from something to do with baseball. John hadn't ever taken the time to notice that baseball was all Christian was into, much like he didn't know Clara was a performer like her aunt. Eduardo had his sights on engineering, that he knew.

Once Madeline had let them into the house, she and Arianna went on like a couple of little girls at a slumber party. He'd heard Zach mention this phenomenon with Arianna and Regan, and Madeline was as much their sister as Carlos was their brother. He figured he was in for a long night, and that hot kiss they'd shared before they left home was more than likely forgotten.

The moment Carlos had seen him sitting at the table with the women, he'd pulled a beer from the fridge and handed it to him.

"C'mon, I have a pool table in the basement."

John followed, happy to have the distraction.

When they made it to the basement, Carlos began to rack the balls. "You might be here all night if those two get to talking."

"I figured as much."

"Madeline has missed Arianna. I'm glad she moved back."

John twisted the top from his beer and took a sip. "I think she is too."

Carlos took the holder off the balls carefully and exchanged it on the rack for a pool cue. "She hasn't heard anything else from Alexander Hamilton, has she?"

"I don't think so. I'm not sure what his motivation in scaring the hell out of her was, but it worked."

Carlos hit the balls and sent them rolling. "Solids." He lined up another shot. "I tell you what. If the man comes near my sisters, or my family, they'll be locking me up for a very long time."

He understood that sentiment. "I've done business with him a few times. I know four years ago Zach had all intentions of sending me to that job. I'm glad it didn't pan out."

Carlos laid the stick on the table and picked up his beer. Obviously the game was a distraction to get John in the basement. That was just as fine.

"You don't really think he wants Regan's baby, do you? The one she gave up, I mean."

"I think the Keller family stopped him from his intentions, and he's a vengeful man."

Carlos shook his head. "I never did like Curtis telling him they both died. But it made him go away. Regan needed that."

"She never kept in touch with the adoptive family?"

"No. She never even looked at the baby. Curtis is the only one who ever saw her." He shrugged. "Seems like a long time ago."

"Wasn't really."

Carlos took a pull from his beer. "Nope, sure wasn't."

Arianna knew she'd made Clara's night by telling her the news. Madeline had screamed aloud, too. It was going to be a wonderful production, and she couldn't wait to get started.

But, at that moment, she was digging into a cherry pie slice at Village Inn, and it was heaven.

She looked up to see John nursing a cup of coffee and staring at her.

"What?" she asked with her mouth full.

"You're beautiful when you're enjoying things."

She swallowed the large piece she'd shoved in her mouth and wiped off her lips. "You're one of those men, huh? The kind that feed women sweets just to see them devour it?"

John shrugged and smiled from behind his mug.

Arianna loaded her fork with a much smaller bite. "I'll have to remember to keep going to yoga, or you'll make me fat."

John sipped his coffee. "Clara seemed excited about *Annie*."

"Oh, she is." She swallowed the next bite and then washed it down with her bitter and cold coffee. "I told you it was what she'd want. And did you hear about Christian? He's going to be playing varsity, and he's only a freshman."

"Pretty talented family."

"Well, don't get me started on Ed. He's the smartest kid I know. If Zach keeps him around, I'll guarantee you Ed will be running the place."

John set down his mug, but it was his face that grabbed hold of her attention. Something was on his mind, and he didn't know how to talk about it. She'd seen it before.

"What's bothering you?"

John let out a breath. "You and your family."

That wasn't a positive statement, and she couldn't imagine where he'd go with it.

"Something wrong with my family?"

"No. No." He tried to ease back in his seat, but he wasn't comfortable. She figured John Forrester hadn't talked so much in his whole life, and now he was having deep conversations on a daily basis. She'd ease him into it.

"My family is very important to me."

"I know. In fact, when you were talking about offering Clara the part, your eyes lit up."

"My nieces and nephews are my life."

He nodded and reached for her hands across the table and held them. "That's what I'm trying to get to. How can you not want to have children?"

Her heartbeat began beating extremely hard in her chest. "Why do you ask?"

"I think you'd be a fantastic mother."

Which way was this going? He hadn't wanted kids. She hadn't wanted kids. That was part of the charm that was their relationship. Which one of them was now causing the problem?

Arianna pursed her lips together. "Do you want kids?"

"I'm fifty-three years old."

"I'm not sure that was an answer to my question."

He held her hands tighter. "I just think that you'd be so good at having them. You shouldn't give that up."

"Do you want kids?" She reiterated her question.

This time he shrugged, and that made her heart rate go even faster. It was very uncomfortable.

"John, what are you trying to say to me? You want to have a baby?"

The tense look on his face softened. "Can you imagine? By the time they were thirty, I'd be eighty-three."

"You're freaking me out. What are you talking about?"

He lifted her hands to his lips and gently placed a kiss on her knuckles. "No, I don't want kids of my own. I gave that desire up years ago. But you are still young enough to have them, and if you wanted them, I wouldn't run away."

She let her shoulders drop. "I don't want kids. I thought you knew that."

"But you love your nieces and nephews so much…"

"Yes, I do." She scooted out of her side of the booth and walked around the table to sit next to him. "They are my world, just as my brothers and sister are. I don't want some big wedding with flower girls and ring bearers either."

"You're sure?"

"You asked me when we first tumbled on my bed if I would commit to you. That's what I did. John, I don't want a wedding dress. I never have. I don't want children. I never have. But I have grown very fond of you."

"Okay." He kissed her on the cheek. "I didn't mean to upset you. I just didn't want you to give up something that might someday be important."

"You're all I want. Stay with me forever?"

"I promise."

Just to prove he did love a woman with her mouth full of pie, John had bought one for them to take home.

Arianna had scolded him, but he'd seen her break off a piece of crust and eat it before she expended him in bed and then fell asleep.

As he watched her dream, he thought about his ex-wife. She was nothing like the woman wrapped in his arms, and he supposed that was why everything now was so perfect.

His ex-wife had a family now. It had been something she'd wanted, and he hadn't been against it. It just hadn't happened. Fate was sometimes generous—no matter how it played itself out.

He was happy for her, even if he hadn't seen her in the nearly ten years since she'd taken everything he'd ever saved. She must have needed it more, he always told himself.

Of course, he'd never been happier than when he'd moved into the basement of Arianna's house and given most of his furniture to Simone when she'd moved to Nashville. He never would have imagined he'd be living upstairs, wrapping his arms around the only other woman, other than his ex-wife, who had ever occupied his mind.

John had been serious about the baby, too. If she'd wanted one, he'd make sure she had one. He'd be a fantastic father. That part he was certain of. But he was just as content to not have children. He, too, adored all of her nieces and nephews. And she was right. If Zach kept Eduardo active in the company, he could see him working the deals and designing the builds just as Zach had done.

Marriage. Now that seemed to be another factor weighing in on his mind.

He was going to buy her the biggest, gaudiest diamond he could find. She deserved that more than any woman he'd ever known. And who wouldn't want to find that wrapped up for their fortieth birthday?

The dilemma was should he attach a proposal with it?

Construction continued on the theater, and Arianna was planning a grand opening performance. She'd been making lists of different classes she could offer when they opened and what kinds of performances she'd be putting together. There were days when she'd wake when John left for work and she'd be sitting in the same place in front of her computer when he came back. There was a lot of planning that went into a new business.

She'd sent off for her business licenses and opened a bank account. The insurance agent had called her at least four times in the past few weeks to tell her he'd been to the site and was always making sure the insurance would be enough on the building.

There had been a few afternoons she'd picked Clara up from school, and they'd gone to the music store to pick up some sheet music to work on. It would never cease to amaze her how much alike they were, and yet, they weren't, technically, even blood related.

It also hadn't gone unnoticed that her fortieth birthday was quickly approaching. The few lines around her eyes reminded her that she wasn't getting any younger, but she'd never been happier.

She was also sure the entire Keller/Benson clan was up to something because no one had talked to her in almost a week.

Arianna wasn't one to ruin surprises—if there was one. She wasn't one to complain if there wasn't one either. Though she'd like them all to at least take her out to dinner.

As she started the coffeepot brewing, she planned out her day. Today she'd find a place to hold auditions for her grand opening event. It would be theatrical, but on a small scale.

When her phone rang, she pulled it from her pocket and answered it.

"Hello." Her voice was song-like as she reached for a mug out of the cupboard.

"The theater looks nice."

Arianna switched her phone to her other ear. She didn't recognize the person, but she hadn't looked at the ID either. "I'm sorry, who is this?"

"It won't always look so nice."

A chill ran down Arianna's spine. "Who are you? What do you want?"

"Don't be stupid. You know what I want."

She set the mug down on the counter and tucked her shaking hand in her pocket. "You need to just go away."

"Your sister is a disgrace. You can't protect her forever."

"Leave us alone. Please. We don't have anything for you."

"She will pay for the lies. Your brother will pay for the lies. *You* will pay."

The line went dead, and Arianna fell to the floor when her knees buckled beneath her.

It could have been an hour. It could have been ten minutes. Arianna wasn't sure. She'd been paralyzed on the floor—shaking, crying, oblivious to everything else.

Her mind had only cleared when John opened the back door, called her name, and ran to her.

Now she sat at the kitchen table, and John handed her a cup of hot tea. She hated tea. Why did she even have it in the cupboard?

He watched her as she forced herself to take a sip. His face was hard. His brows narrowed, his lips were tight, and his face was a flush of red that could only mean anger.

She hadn't had to tell him much. He knew. He'd called the police and her family, but only after he'd called Zach and put him in motion to get to Regan.

Arianna knew that she was about to face the wrath of John Forrester. She set down the mug, placed her hands in her lap, and waited.

"You can't be weak. What if he'd been here? What if..."

"He wasn't."

"The last thing I'd expect from you is to find you on the floor."

"I'm sorry. This isn't my style. He just caught me off guard..."

"And that's what he wanted." He raked his fingers through his hair. "If he can frazzle you, he can get to Regan. Don't you see that?"

She really hadn't until he said it aloud.

"Jesus, Arianna, I can't lose you, and if you're going to play with fire then we're all going to get burned."

Now she was angry. She pushed up from her seat. "How has this become my fault? I came back to Nashville to be near my family. He's stalking me. I didn't ask for this."

"Are you sure?"

That had crossed the line. She kicked back the chair and charged him. She'd smack him, punch him, and stop him from talking such nonsense. But he was quick. He caught her hands.

"Calm down."

"Calm down? Are you kidding me?" She pulled her hands from his hold. "You're accusing me of doing…something to provoke this."

He touched her arm, and she jerked away. "Actually, I was seeing how you'd react so I'd know you didn't."

She crossed her arms over her chest. "Not very trustworthy of you."

"He's not going to hurt Regan or the boys. Zach will see to that."

"He's going to try."

John shook his head. "He's not going to make it."

The pounding at the back door had Arianna jumping back. John turned and opened the door to Curtis who nearly knocked him over as he rushed past him.

"What is with you?" Curtis grabbed her arms. "I've watched Regan come through the hospital twice. Once she nearly died at the hands of that monster and then again when you," he turned and pointed at John, "fired that S.O.B. who tried to rape and kill her."

She watched as John fisted his hands at his side.

Curtis turned back to her. "Now you've collected some maniac, too? What did you do in New York?"

Arianna's jaw dropped as she stared at her brother. "I had nothing to do with Alexander Hamilton. I didn't do this."

"You had to have done something to have some guy stalking you."

"Some guy? He's after Regan."

"No." Curtis let go of her and shook his head. "Simone just got off the phone with her mother. Alexander Hamilton is in Paris."

CHAPTER THIRTEEN

John paced the floor of his basement apartment—now his *man cave*.

Again, the police had nothing to offer. An untraceable prank phone call wasn't their first priority.

Arianna had locked herself in her bedroom as soon as Curtis had left. The only thing left for him to do was to wait until she was ready to talk, but Curtis had brought up some points. Who had Arianna been involved with that would do this to her?

He heard her stomp down the stairs, and he waited. Soon the noises were coming from the kitchen. It was time to face her and ask his own questions.

John took the stairs slowly. It had been a long time since he had had to deal with a woman's feelings. Truth was, he wasn't great at it, and with lack of practice, he couldn't expect that this was going to go well.

Arianna was wrapped in her robe, leaning against the counter, sipping from a bottle of water. He couldn't read her so he just watched.

"Forrester, if you're going to come up here on tip toe and stand quietly, you're in for a world of hurt."

He tucked his thumbs into his front pockets and rocked back on his heels. "How's that?"

"I'm a screamer. When I'm mad, I have a tendency to scream, yell, and throw things. So this is your choice. You can disappear back into your cave, or you can see this very ugly side of me."

He considered her words and then walked to the kitchen table. He pulled out a chair and sat down. "Considering you've been quietly upstairs for the last hour, I'm going to assume anything being broken over my head would have happened already. So here I am. Let the words fly."

Her eyes widened. "That's it? You're just going to sit there and let me have at it?"

"Did I make you mad? Are you mad at me?"

"I…well, no."

"You're mad at Alexander Hamilton. You're mad at Curtis. Hell, you're probably mad at that inspector that made me change out that light switch. But, the point is, I haven't done anything to warrant you walking out on me, so I'm here to let you do what you need to do."

She stomped her bare foot against the floor. "You're ruining what could be a real good fit."

"I'm sorry. How can I help?"

She crossed her arms over her chest, but the smile she'd been trying to force away snuck through. "Damn you. I wanted to scream at you."

"And I'm offering the opportunity for you to do that."

She shook her head. "I think I have a better idea." She let her arms drop to her sides as she walked right up to John. With just one finger, she pulled the ties apart on her robe and then shrugged it off of her shoulders.

He could smell the lavender scent from her skin. She'd soaked her worries away in a hot bath. Now she stood there before him naked and beautiful.

This was the part of the relationship that made the fits of anger and insecurity worth it. As he pulled her down on his lap and pressed his mouth against her, he knew it didn't matter who she'd been with in the past. It didn't matter who was messing with them and keeping them on edge. What mattered was they would be together forever.

Arianna lay in bed, her eyes wide open, the room dark. John breathed a steady rhythm next to her.

She didn't care what Curtis said. There was no one she'd been with who would stalk her. She'd been the one who heard the words the man spoke. It didn't matter that Simone's mother said that Alexander Hamilton was in Paris. Arianna knew that he was the one trying to scare her and her family, and he was doing a good job.

She knew what he was capable of. And if Simone had been right about his wife leaving him and his loss of fortune, wouldn't he be vengeful? After all, he'd tried to kill Regan and her baby. This wasn't a man who had much fear.

On the other hand, he didn't have what she had. She had a family that would fight to the very end, and if a fight was what he wanted, then that would be what he would get.

But until he showed his face, she'd carry her gun in her purse. She'd keep her sister close. And at night she'd sleep in the arms of the man she loved because, no matter what Alexander Hamilton said or did, she knew John Forrester would never leave her.

As always, Arianna stood at the steps which led up to the theater the next morning. Her grande, skinny caramel latte warmed her throat as she took a sip and looked up at the building her family had bought her. They might all have had a hand in owning it, but it was hers to make great.

John opened the front door and walked toward her. She couldn't help but smile when she saw him. He wasn't the man she had thought she'd spend the rest of her life with, but it had worked out that way.

His hair shimmered in the early morning sun which was filtered by the clouds. It was obvious he did most of his work inside during the winter as his tanned skin was paler.

She'd never tell him, but the creases around his eyes were one of his sexiest features.

"You know, I have coffee in my trailer at all times. You don't have to spend good money on a fancy cup," he said as he leaned in to kiss her.

"Let's say it reminds me of New York." She sipped her coffee again. "I'm meeting with a minister today."

"You have plans you haven't told me about?"

She laughed easily knowing he'd see right through her. "I'm going to rent a church basement for a few weeks to get my *act* together."

"Funny." He took her coffee from her and took a sip. He swallowed hard and wrinkled up his nose. "You really should save your money."

"You're too manly for my coffee."

"Damn straight." He gave her a nod. "So what are you putting together?"

"Clara is going to help me after school, and an old friend and I are going to put together a musical review. I want to do it for a grand opening. When you give me the date, that is."

"Oh, I see. You're trying to pull a number from me, and here I thought you were being sexy in your mittens and long coat."

"So, what do you think?"

"Honey, this place is a mess. Let me talk to Zach, but I still think you're looking at July."

She let out a grunt. "Well, then it will be the most spectacular music review ever."

"I have no doubt."

She moved in closer to him. "You know what you and I haven't done as a couple yet?"

A tight grin formed on his lips. "You mean we've left something out?"

"A vacation."

His shoulders pushed back, and his smile disappeared. "I thought you wanted this place done."

"Construction foremans don't get vacations?"

"Fishing weekends."

"Zach could cover."

"He's busy."

"We could hold everything off a week."

"Doesn't work that way."

If she let her anger, which was stirring inside her, get the better of her, she'd crush the cup in her hand. Instead, she took a breath and backed away. "I'll settle for a fishing weekend then."

Arianna turned back toward her car and quickly drove away while he stood there watching her.

The woman was thick-headed. He pinched the bridge of his nose. John had already sunk his savings into the dilapidated building and had arranged to meet Regan at a jeweler to pick out a ring for her. The last thing he'd wanted her to think was he'd take her away somewhere, but that was the plan. In fact, had she walked into his trailer and seen his computer screen, she'd probably see the confirmation. Two round trip tickets to San Francisco.

A few more weeks of secrets and he swore he'd never keep another.

The church's basement was small, but it would work for the time being. Madeline dropped Clara off after school, and when she jumped up and down because there was a stage, that was all the validation Arianna needed.

"This is almost as cool as the theater," Clara squealed as she danced around on the stage.

Arianna pulled up a folding chair and sat down. She just watched as Clara created, unbothered by the audience of one.

That had been her once. Life was Arianna's stage, and she was the star. Oh, her mother would have fits over the tall tales she could weave, but she always knew when they were the truth and when they were her wild imagination.

Her very first role had come when she was five. She was a tomato, and a very convincing one at that.

By the time she was in high school, the drama department belonged to her. There wasn't a production she didn't carry.

Sitting on the side lines would be much different and require as much discipline. But it was someone else's turn to be the star, she just felt it.

Arianna eased back in the chair as Clara messed with an amplifier on the stage and tapped on the microphone. It wasn't a song she'd ever heard. She assumed it had been created right there on the spot. But it was beautiful.

The song, the sound, mimicked her life as it was right now—beautiful. She'd run from New York in a panic. John's handsome face meeting her at the airport was exactly the calm she'd needed. How was it that she'd run away right to where she was supposed to be?

"What did you think, Auntie?" Clara spoke into the microphone.

"I think you have the voice of an angel."

"I was thinking Faith Hill."

"Perhaps even better." Arianna stood up and walked to the stage. "Is that who you want to sound like?"

Clara shrugged. "I think that would be fun—to be a country artist."

"Then maybe you will be someday. What do you say we go to get some ice cream and make some notes on our show?"

Clara turned off the amplifier and jumped down off the stage. "I say you're on."

She walked out of the church basement with her arm around the shoulders of her niece. There was a grand comfort there, but John's questions about children zipped back through her mind. Would this comfort be enough?

CHAPTER FOURTEEN

John was rethinking his decision to buy Arianna a ring. A dog might have been easier. She'd love some mutt. But this…

He'd invited Regan to help him pick the perfect ring for her sister. She, in turn, invited Madeline and Simone.

John knew he could have dealt with Regan. He was used to that. Madeline was soft spoken, and her opinion wasn't too grand. But why had Regan thought it necessary to invite Simone of all people?

He was used to Simone Pierpont, but that had been in dealings with her as the face of Pierpont Oil, gaining investors in builds. Picking out jewelry? He should have just bought the dog.

"John, do you know anything about her taste?" Simone scanned the cases of rings.

"Yes. She's simple."

Regan chuckled, but kept her eyes on the rings.

Simone shook her head. "I think we are off. We should move from the wedding bands."

With that she walked across the store. Both Regan and Madeline exchanged glances and hurried after her. John, on the other hand, looked down at the rings he thought were perfectly nice. Sure, it wasn't going to be a *wedding* ring, but it had the same value.

"John."

He looked up to see Regan waving him over. There was a look on her face that frightened him.

He couldn't have been more surprised when all three women pointed to one ring in the case.

"This one," Regan said quietly.

"It's her," Madeline chimed in.

"It is brilliant," was Simone's addition.

"It's blue," was his own opinion, and that had all three women laughing.

Simone, of course, moved in next to him and pointed at the ring through the glass. "It is an oval shaped sapphire with two round diamonds beside it. It is set in white gold, which is very nice. Sapphire represents sincerity, truth, and faithfulness—which is what you are looking for, right?"

He knew his mouth hung open, and he nodded.

Madeline shook her head and looked at Simone. "How do you know all of that?"

"I used to own a lot of jewelry." She laughed and then looked down at the simple solitaire diamond which adorned her finger. "None of my jewels from before mattered at all. This ring—this simple ring—means more than any fortune."

The look of contentment on Simone's face was exactly what he wanted to see on Arianna's.

"Ya'll think this is the one?"

The three women nodded together.

"You're sure I shouldn't go with something traditional like a wedding ring?"

Regan smiled. "She doesn't want marriage. This," she pointed to the ring, "says you gave some very sincere thought to it."

Regan stayed with him after the others had left. She'd tried on the ring with the sapphire and a few others, but John knew they were right. The sapphire ring with the diamonds was the best.

As the sales woman cleaned it up and put it in a box, he sat at the counter with Regan, contemplating what he'd done.

"You look like someone is going to shoot you," she said.

"Sorry. I wasn't even this nervous when I proposed to my ex-wife."

"Arianna makes you nervous?"

"Extremely, but in a very good way. I don't even know if that makes sense." And he was tired of no longer making sense.

"It makes perfect sense. You love her, and you want everything to be right."

"But already everything is way beyond where I thought we'd be. I had no intentions of having…" he stopped, realizing it wasn't appropriate to continue the conversation.

However, Regan's grin told him he had nothing to worry about. "I know you've had sex, John. She'd been planning that since Carlos's wedding to Kathy."

"How is it I'm the only one that didn't know that?"

"You're too good for your own good."

"I wasn't going to mess things up between my boss's sister-in-law and myself."

"Doesn't seem messed up to me."

She was right. It was almost perfect in its very mixed up way. "They aren't going to tell her about the ring, are they?"

"Madeline and Simone? Of course not. Those two love surprises."

John rubbed the back of his neck. "I planned a trip to San Francisco, too."

Regan slapped his shoulder. "You've gone all out, haven't you?"

He shrugged. "Seems like too much."

"Are you kidding me? She'll eat it up."

He nodded then let out a deep breath. "I had actually contemplated asking her to marry me."

The smile on Regan's face diminished. "Do you think that's a good idea?"

"Not anymore I don't."

Regan readjusted her purse on her shoulder and then looked up at him. "She's never wanted it. Marriage, that is."

"She's mentioned that."

"Then don't do it. Is that what you want? Marriage? Babies?"

Before he gave her an answer, he gave it some thought. "I thought it was for a moment, but…"

"John, if that's what you want, you have to make some serious decisions."

He didn't like the severity of her tone. What was so bad about marriage and babies—and why was he questioning it? That wasn't what he wanted—he didn't think.

The saleswoman handed him his purchase, and he and Regan walked out into the plaza where the store was located.

Regan turned right to him. "Are you going to propose?"

"Why would she turn me down?"

"She doesn't want marriage."

"But why is it different than what we have now?"

"It just is." She let her shoulders drop. "I don't know why she's so shy about it. She believes in commitment. She believes in forever and family."

"But a piece of paper that signifies it is the deal breaker?"

Regan looked around as if she were looking for answers. "Yes."

John took the ring downstairs and tucked it away. The stage was almost done, under direct orders from Zach himself. Another week and they'd surprise her with a grand fortieth birthday celebration.

Until then, he had to keep secrets and he hated that.

He'd hoped to be back upstairs before she was home, but it didn't work that way. The front door slammed, and he heard her purse and bag drop to the floor.

It was time to just smile and pretend as though earlier that morning she hadn't wanted to fly away.

John walked up the stairs. He could hear her now in the kitchen. As he rounded the corner, he caught a glimpse of her standing there holding out a beer for him, but what took him by surprise was the lack of clothing she had on.

It was hard to imagine that in the few minutes she'd been home she'd changed into such an *outfit*.

John took the beer. "Thank you," he said, but the words croaked out.

"Do you like it?"

What was not to like? A few pieces of fabric covered only very intimate parts of the body he'd committed to memory.

"I like it."

She moved in closer to him and wrapped her arms around his neck. "Good. I brought Chinese food."

His blood supply had drained from his brain which only made him dizzy when she changed the subject.

"Are you eating in that?" He gave her a long glance.

"One of the best things about Chinese food is that it warms up nice." At that point she grabbed the front of his shirt and pulled him through the kitchen to the living room. She took the beer from his hand, set it on the coffee table and pushed him back onto the couch.

These were reasons to never have children. Not every man could have the woman of his dreams, barely dressed, force him into a very comfortable position on the couch.

Arianna swung her leg over him and positioned herself above his hips.

"Your choice, Forrester. I can keep this little thing on, or you can take it off."

"You're going to make me think about something right now? You're torturing me."

A sexy, evil grin crossed her lips. "Good. Now let's see what else I can do to you."

Arianna figured she'd taken him by surprise in more ways than one. Except for gasps and moans, John Forrester hadn't said a word in nearly two hours. Now propped up on pillows eating cold Chinese food from cartons with the evening news playing on the television in the corner, she watched as he nourished himself. His chest still heaved as though he couldn't get enough breath in his lungs.

Yep, she'd worn the man out.

That had been the plan. She'd acted like a child when he said he couldn't take her on a trip. She didn't like it, but she'd accept it for now.

It was given to her, under good authority, that he was a lover of a great fishing trip. So she'd taken it upon herself to book a guided trip, not too far from home.

They had rushed into everything else, even though they'd met four years ago. So she had to learn that commitment, living together, and promising each other the rest of their lives were big decisions that they'd forced upon each other in less than a month. There were still things to learn about each other. But one thing she had learned about John Forrester was that he was quiet, passive, and easy to please. Something she knew about herself—she was bossy. Arianna Keller got what she wanted when she wanted it, so John would have to adapt.

CHAPTER FIFTEEN

It had been a rush job, but John stood where the front row of seats would be bolted down and admired the stage.

Zach and Regan stood to his side, both quietly in awe as well.

"I can't believe it's the same place." Regan kept Spencer close to her chest with a small blanket over his head to keep him safe from the dust.

Zach held tight to Tyler's hand. The little boy watched the workers fixing the sconces on the walls. His little hard hat shielded his eyes.

Zach put a supportive hand on John's shoulder. "I know you're a wizard at coming in under budget and on time, but this is crazy. You'll have this place up and ready far before July."

"I hope so, but I'm not moving my schedule and I'm sure not telling Arianna that." He shook his head. "She'll have a production planned."

Regan smiled up at him. "Clara can't stop talking about it."

"Neither can her aunt. She's proud of what she's already put together. I haven't seen it yet, but it's going to be one hell of a production."

"She wouldn't have it any other way."

John removed his hard hat and ran his hand over his head. "I guess the stage is done and they'll rehang the curtain tomorrow, so you can now commence with your party plans."

"She's going to be so surprised."

"If I may ask you," he said as he turned to her, "please hurry. That ring is making me antsy just having it around, and I don't like keeping secrets from her."

"You're a true gentleman, John Forrester."

"I don't feel like one. So hurry."

By the time John pulled up to the house, Regan had called him six times with details to the party. He guessed he was supposed to be grateful for all the information, but, in reality, all he wanted was to show up. So far he knew the invitations were being printed, Audrey was working with a caterer, the first party rental place fell through so Regan had contacted another, and he'd need to have the lighting ready in two weeks. That part he'd heard and was very efficient on.

When John opened the door to the house, he was a bit surprised to hear laugher coming from the kitchen. He approached slowly. A woman with a friend, whose car he hadn't seen, was a dangerous thing.

"Oh, John, I didn't hear you." Arianna stood up and gave him a loud, wet kiss right on the lips. Then she turned to the other woman seated at the table. "John, this is April. We worked together in New York. She's a choreographer."

The woman stood up and held her hand out for him. "I've been hearing a lot about you, John. It's nice to finally meet you."

John shook the woman's hand, and the shake wasn't dainty. "Nice to meet you."

"April surprised me by stopping by this afternoon. I was telling her about the theater."

"I can't wait to see it." April's eyes lit up as brightly as Arianna's when she mentioned it.

Arianna gently touched his arm. "Are you up for going out to dinner with two beautiful women?"

He'd been hoping to tangle one of them in the sheets, but that didn't seem to be in the cards. "You bet. Let me get a shower."

Arianna watched John take the steps. He was tired. This was one of those true tests in a relationship, and so far he was passing.

April sat back down at the table. "He's as handsome as you said he was."

"Isn't he?" Arianna took her seat, picked up her glass of wine and finished it off.

"The age difference between you doesn't bother you?"

"Not in the least. Why should it?"

April shrugged. "Because in thirteen years you'll be his age and he'll be almost seventy."

Arianna had to admit that forty and fifty-three hadn't even caused a bit of concern, but when April put it that way, it did seem extreme.

"I love him. I don't see that changing when he's ninety and I'm seventy-seven." Although, when she said it aloud, fear crept through her veins. He was a bit older than her. She'd better be very sure that she wanted a lifetime commitment and not a marriage license. Likewise, and more importantly, she'd better make sure she really didn't want the children that she'd said she didn't want. Quality time with them would be slipping away. John was already the age most men became grandfathers, and here he was without children. But, on the other hand, since he didn't waste his energy on carpooling and running after kids, his energy was high and, on a younger woman, that hadn't gone unnoticed. Nothing had been lost with his age.

Arianna looked into the bottom of her empty glass. "Would you like more wine?"

"I've never been one to turn down more wine. Especially if a nice looking man is going to drive us to dinner."

John stepped into the shower. He hoped the hot water would wash away his tension. He was sure he wasn't supposed to hear April ask Arianna what she thought about their age difference.

Arianna's answer hadn't bothered him. In fact, he thought she handled it very well. But it was the few seconds of hesitation that had gotten to him.

What was he doing? She deserved someone her own age. He had nothing to offer a relationship at this point.

For most of his life his job had been the most important thing to him. He'd always been the man Zach and Tyler Benson could count on. They'd sent him all over the world to oversee projects.

Perhaps a relationship would hold him back, too.

With a woman at home, he couldn't travel as he had. Those jobs could take a few months at a time.

Wouldn't she want someone who could offer her more? He was too simple. The only thing he knew about theater was how to build one.

He hadn't finished college, and he'd only squeaked out of high school.

He lathered shampoo in his hands and ran his fingers through his hair.

Was this why his wife had left him? His job was more important than she was?

In the past month he'd already put in more work with Arianna than he had in nearly twenty years of marriage.

John rinsed the soap from his hair. It had been his fault. He'd driven his wife into the arms of another man—a man who would be there for her and not leave for months at a time. This other man gave her the children John had never wanted.

The knock at the door had him dropping the soap from his hand.

"You doing alright? You've been in there forever," Arianna's sweet voice carried through the steam filled room.

"I guess I hadn't noticed. I'll be out in a few minutes."

"I thought we could go for bar-b-que and then maybe take April by the theater to look at it."

Just hearing her speak to him put him at ease. He hadn't treated his wife the way he treated Arianna because, he realized at that moment, he'd never loved her as he loved Arianna.

"You bet. I'll be down in a few."

April had a lot of energy, and John could see she even wore Arianna out.

She'd had one story after another during dinner. If he wasn't driving, he'd have had four more beers.

That wasn't to say she wasn't a nice woman. She just talked a lot.

He was pleased, though, that she'd had the same enthusiasm when she'd tasted the food at Steve's. It was the best, and most people agreed on that.

After dinner he drove to the theater.

"So, Arianna, what are your plans for opening night?"

"We're going to have a soft opening, and my niece and I are putting something together. This will be held for my friends, family, and the community. But our first production will be *Annie*, in honor of the first musical I ever saw and it was at the theater."

"That'll be wonderful. You don't suppose Eric will come, do you?"

Arianna didn't answer right away, and John watched as her jaw tightened and she clasped her fingers in her lap.

"I can't imagine why he would."

John was grateful they arrived in front of the theater when they did. The tension in the car had become nearly toxic. Aside from that, he knew he'd get no sleep tonight. There was a lot to hash out with this woman he loved.

He put the car in park and unbuckled his seat belt. April was already out of the car and staring up at the building, which wouldn't get a new coat of paint for a week.

John touched Arianna's arm. "You okay?"

"Doing great." She smiled through gritted teeth.

He didn't take her demeanor personally. He assumed with the story of Eric would come some reason April made her so tense.

John stepped out of the car and Arianna followed. He walked up the steps to unlock the door.

"Arianna, this place is creepy."

"Not once you're inside. Besides it's under construction. In a few months, it will be amazing."

April made a noise of acceptance and followed after John as he stepped inside to turn on the lights.

A moment later, the few lights illuminated the lobby. John looked at Arianna. The glimmer was back in her eyes. No matter what this girl knew about the woman he loved, she couldn't diminish the love she had for what she was building—what they were building.

"So...what's this supposed to look like?" April questioned the run down lobby.

"This is our lobby. Over there is concessions. And over there," she turned and pointed to the other side of the room, "is my office."

April nodded. "Can we go into the theater?"

"Of course."

Arianna led her through the large doors in the center of the room, and John followed.

The few lights that still came on with the switch, along with the work lights he'd turned on, gave the theater an eerie glow.

April only took a few steps through the door.

"When do you get your seats?"

John stepped up next to her. "We put those in last."

"Oh."

Arianna was hurrying toward the stage. "They just finished the stage. Isn't it beautiful?"

John heard her gasp, and she turned toward him.

"The curtains are back."

"And better than ever." He walked through the theater to stand next to her. "Whoever Regan found to clean and repair them did a great job. I don't know much about curtains, but I know they look great."

Arianna covered her mouth and John could see tears surface in her eyes, but they weren't sad tears.

"Thank you."

He touched her face and looked into her eyes. "I love you. Everything here is going to be perfect."

"I do believe it is."

April had made her way to the stage and was walking up the side steps. "There's a lot of room here. I think you'll be able to do some big productions."

John thought it might have been the most positive statement the woman had made all night long.

April walked out to the center of the stage. "I'm sorry, honey, but this place creeps me out. I feel like I'm being watched."

Arianna laughed and followed her up to the stage. "Isn't that what's supposed to happen in old buildings?"

"I'm serious. It sounds like someone is..." but April didn't finish her sentence.

Suddenly, from the catwalk, a sandbag attached to a rope swung through the air.

Arianna pushed April out of the way and nearly landed right on top of her as the bag dangled right where they'd been standing.

John heard footsteps, and he hurried up the stairs as the backdoor to the theater opened and slammed shut.

He hurried to the door, but when he opened it and looked outside, the person was gone.

John rushed back to the women who sat on the stage in each other's arms, panting.

"Someone was here," he said.

April lifted her arm and looked at her elbow. "I told you I thought someone was watching me."

Arianna shifted her glance to John. The gratitude which had filled her eyes before had been replaced with fear.

CHAPTER SIXTEEN

There had been near silence all the way to April's hotel and home. John was furious. Someone was messing around; and it was bound to kill someone. He'd be damned if it were Arianna or Regan, or anyone he knew.

She was keeping secrets from him, and he didn't like it. His ex-wife had kept her share of secrets, and he hadn't taken too lightly to them either.

Though John loved Arianna, he wouldn't be betrayed.

He tightened his grip on the steering wheel. Who was he kidding? Doubt had been placed in his head by Curtis and April. Names and situations had been dropped, and now he was second guessing the woman he loved. Was this the plan of the bastard who was chasing her?

John pulled her car into the driveway and put it in park.

"So who is Eric?" He tried to keep his voice calm, but there was no calm in his entire body.

Arianna sat in the passenger seat with her hands in her lap, gripping her purse. "He was a director in New York that I lived with for a while."

"How long ago?"

"We broke up about six months ago."

John nodded. "Not that long ago."

"Long enough."

She reached for the door handle, and he reached for her. "Did you love him?"

"What?"

"I'm not playing games with you. Did you love him?"

Arianna let go of the door and turned to him. "Yes. Yes I thought I loved him. Guess what? I was wrong."

This time she managed to push open the door, but John quickly climbed out of the car and hurried around to the other side. He reached for her and spun her toward him.

"Just like that? You live with a man and then you decide he's no good for you?"

"Were you there? No. So don't stand here and talk to me like that."

"Arianna, it seems like you're just changing cities and men."

He kept an eye on her hand which tightened around the strap of her purse. "Don't you ever talk to me like that again. Do you hear me?"

"Then tell me about him. Why would April assume he'd come here to see you? Why is someone following you? Why is someone trying to hurt you? Give me some damn answers."

"I'm telling you who it is. He wants to hurt Regan and Curtis for lying to him."

"Hamilton?"

"Yes."

"Curtis said he's in Paris."

"I don't care what he says. The man is trying to hurt my family, and I have no doubt that he was behind what happened tonight."

"Why would Curtis doubt his fiancée?"

"It wasn't his wife that gave us that information."

John ran his hands over his head. "You think he set it up somehow for her to tell us that?"

"I don't know." She pushed past him and up the front steps.

Her fingers were red, and he could see she was having a hard time with the key. He took it from her and unlocked the door.

Without a word she moved past him, through the living room and into the kitchen.

When he walked through the doorway, something flew at him. He moved out of the way only to find it was a kitchen towel, but she was right. When she was mad she threw things, and she was just about to start to yell. The vein in her forehead was bulging.

This was going to be a long night.

Arianna tried to breathe through the anger, but it was bigger than she was.

"Eric was a married S.O.B. who didn't bother to tell me he had a wife and kids upstate. So the bastard lived with me. Slept with me. He told me he loved me and that I was everything he'd ever wanted."

She paced the kitchen. "He didn't love me."

Tears were burning her eyes, and she hated that it all mattered. She hated him—so why cry? Because she'd thought it was real.

"I can guarantee this isn't Eric who is stalking me. He's stupid, but he's not vicious."

"He could be."

"But he's not." She wiped the tears from her cheeks. "I had a call from Hamilton a while ago, and he specifically told me that Regan and Curtis would pay for what they did to him. Simone told me his wife left him, and he's lost his fortune."

She looked up at John, who was coming right at her. For the first time since she'd met the man, she was actually afraid of him.

Arianna backed against the counter and braced herself when he grabbed her arms. "You can't just keep this stuff to yourself. Lives are at stake. Your life!"

She had gone speechless. He was right. She couldn't be silent about it. Tonight was a fine example of how close this crazy person was—no matter who they were.

John let go of her and took a step back.

"I'm sorry." He scrubbed his hands over his face. "I will not lose you to my anger or to this mad man. I have never loved anyone as much as I love you, and this is driving me crazy."

John had said so much in that one sentence that she couldn't quite wrap her head around it. She'd never loved anyone as much as she loved John. And damn it, she didn't want to die at the hands of some crazed man, whoever he was.

"What do we do?" Her voice was soft—weak.

"You're going to have to be with me or Regan at all times."

"Okay."

"I don't want you to be alone, and I don't want you at the theater unless I tell you to be there. Got it?"

She only nodded. It was understood that this was not the time to be a headstrong woman and argue with the man.

"If you're going to meet with Clara, you're going to do it at the theater when I'm there."

She nodded again.

"And damn it, if that phone rings or buzzes or dings again, I want to know about it. You're not helping anyone by hiding it."

Her body shook with anger and fear. She wanted this over. She wanted her freedom back. Most of all, she wanted to know her family was safe.

Arianna was certainly surprised to find John still home when she woke the next morning. He was antsy, too.

He sat at the kitchen table, a cup of coffee in his hand, and his foot tapping a quick rhythm on the floor.

"What are you doing here?"

He looked up at her. "You're coming to work with me."

"Do you really mean I *have* to be with you every minute?"

"I'm sure I didn't stutter. Now go get dressed. I'm late."

Arianna did what had been expected of her.

The ride into work was quiet, but he had allowed her a stop at Starbucks.

John parked behind the theater. Together they walked up the back ramp to the back stage door, but Zach met them before they went inside.

"Your visitor was back," he said, his eyes narrowed on Arianna.

"Our visit…the person who was here last night?"

"Maybe you should just go over to my house and be with Regan. Curtis and Simone are there now."

Arianna fisted her hands on her hips. "I'm not running from this. He wants us to cower."

John stepped up closer. "What did he do?"

Zach let out a deep breath and stepped aside, letting them both in.

Arianna's heart jumped into her throat. Across the brand new stage, in red paint, had been written DIE!

John knew it could be fixed. It all could be fixed, but was it worth it? Maybe it was still worth selling the lot and letting them doze it to the ground.

"Do you want me to take you to Regan's?"

"No. This is our place. I'm not going to let him push us out of it." Arianna turned to John. "You put me to work. I'm here to help in any way I can." She pushed her shoulders back. "There is a grand opening coming up in July, and the musical *Annie* is going to be performed on this stage. So we need to get to work."

For the first time in days, John smiled. "I do believe you mean all that."

"Damn straight I do. Trust me," she opened her purse and let him look inside, "if the bastard shows his face, I'm ready."

John shook his head when he saw the gun. "Do you know how to shoot that thing?"

"I was raised in Tennessee. Doesn't every girl in Tennessee know how?"

He had no doubt.

John had been content with Arianna on site, and she'd actually been an asset. The writing on the stage had been sanded off, by her. She now had a new skill—sander.

She'd eaten burritos from a cooler when the Mexican woman brought them by and sold them for one dollar each. Though she was leery, he'd encouraged her by telling her it was a worksite treat.

He'd seen her in the corner of the theater a few times, on her cell phone with her notebook in hand, jotting down notes.

She needed a place to work.

John had made many trips through the entire theater throughout the day. The lobby was coming along, and the dressing rooms and back stage weren't so run down anymore.

There was an entire crew working to scrape up the floor in the theater so they could patch it up and get it ready for seats.

But the one room that hadn't been attended to was Arianna's office.

There was a special man he was going to put on that job. He looked at his watch and then looked up at the door.

Right on time.

Eduardo walked through the front door of the theater and gave John a wave.

"It's looking nice in here."

"If we could keep the vagrants out," John said.

"Someone's been in here?"

John thought it was better that Eduardo didn't know exactly what had happened, but at least he'd be aware now. "Yeah. Hey, I have a project for you. Come with me."

John led Eduardo to the office where Arianna would run her new empire. It wasn't very big, but it had space for a few people. Right now, however, it was just another junked out room.

"What can you do with this?"

Eduardo looked around the room and his lip snarled. "This is going to be her office, right?"

"Yep."

Eduardo puckered his lips and looked around. John had seen this phenomenon with him before. This was him coming up with something brilliant.

"I'd put in a wall over there." He pointed to the far end of the room. Not to give her another office, but just to give her some privacy. Maybe even put a window in it so she could see the door. I think two desks could go here and maybe a table where she could work on. You know, lay things out. She does that."

John nodded. Yep, she sure did.

Eduardo gave a hum as he looked around more. "The colors need to be vibrant. Creative."

He walked around the room. "Maybe we can add a closet over there." He pointed to the wall. "Just to keep the room organized. You know, she'd have somewhere to put all the papers and scripts. Things like that."

"I think you have a solid grasp on this."

Eduardo looked up at him. "It seems fairly cut and dry."

"Good." John put his hand on Eduardo's shoulder. "You have one week to make this place home for your aunt. It's all yours."

And with that, he left Eduardo in the room, either contemplating beginning or trying to figure out what John had just offered.

When John walked back into the theater, he saw Arianna in the corner and April had showed up. Hands were being waved around, and he knew they were in a serious conversation. Arianna had mentioned an old friend was going to help her put together her musical review. He assumed that meant April. He'd adapt.

As he took another step his cell phone rang. It was Regan.

"Is she okay? What is she doing there?" She shot off questions before he was even able to say hello.

"She's working. This is keeping her mind busy."

"I'm not comfortable with this. Simone just told me her mother thinks that maybe she'd been mistaken about seeing *him* in Paris."

John's hand tightened around the phone. "So it could have been him here last night?"

"Yes."

John squeezed his eyes tight. He wasn't going to let Alexander Hamilton touch another person. He was with Arianna, but he didn't want to live in fear either.

"John, I think we should move the party," she offered.

"What did you have in mind?"

"Audrey and I want to have it here at the house. We've contacted all the guests and told them about the change in plans.

"I don't see that being a problem."

"I'll call her and invite the two of you out for dinner. It'll give her a reason to come out."

John smiled. If this slipped past Arianna, he'd be surprised.

"Sounds like a plan."

April had convinced Arianna to have lunch with her. John conceded as long as he knew where she was and she promised to call when she got to the restaurant and when she left.

She hadn't had someone watch over her that closely since she'd lived with her parents. But it was okay. She didn't want any run-ins with anyone else either.

Arianna sat back in her chair as the waitress set down a salad in front of her and then another in front of April.

April shook out her napkin and placed it in her lap. "So do you know who this crazy stalker of yours is? Is it Eric?"

Arianna picked up her fork and stabbed a piece of lettuce. "I don't think it's Eric. To be honest, I don't think he has it in him. It takes some guts to put something like this together."

"Guts to try and kill someone?"

Arianna swallowed hard. "Yeah."

"I don't know why you're going through with this theater then? I mean, why put yourself in harm's way? I'd find a new career."

Arianna took a bite of her salad. There were many reasons some people were successful and some people failed.

Arianna had always had a dream. And like every dream, there are lots and lots of steps.

Lots of girls have dreams of being an actress. Some wish for it their whole life, and some go after it.

Her mother had driven her to countless voice lessons and dance classes. Her father had videotaped every performance she had since she'd been in preschool.

Arianna had worked her way from the concessions girl to seating patrons and handing out the playbills. She had auditioned for every school play and community event her entire life, and yes, sometimes her name had been on the cut list. And sometimes it was right next to the names *Eliza Doolittle, Rizzo,* and *Ado Annie.*

Blood, sweat and tears went into the career, and now it was changing again. She was in charge. She'd call the shots, and she'd make the lists. This was bigger than she'd ever imagined it could be. The Rockwell Theater would have community events, open mic nights, big time musicals, and yes, her own musicals, which she would write.

How could someone tell her to just give it all up?

No, she'd prevail. And if she had to, she'd use that gun in her purse and turn Alexander Hamilton "from a rooster to a hen in one shot," just as one of her favorite characters, *Doralee Rhodes,* said about her boss. She'd do it.

CHAPTER SEVENTEEN

Arianna fussed with her hair. Winter dried out her curls. She often wondered if her birth mother had hair like hers. Dark and unruly.

It wasn't often that she thought about her birth mother. She didn't remember her at all, but then again, she and Regan had been taken from their birth parents when they were very little. Arianna had only been two.

It was funny to her that she remembered Carlos's family. He'd stopped mentioning them years ago, but she wondered if he still thought of them often. He'd been seven when they'd died. She was sure he still visited their graves when he needed it.

"What's all the fussing in the mirror for? You're usually low maintenance," John said as he leaned against the door jamb.

Arianna yanked on a curl and tried to get it to stay, and then picked up her mascara. "Me? Look at you. Dockers? I didn't even know you owned those. And your shirt isn't flannel."

"So?"

"So, I'd say you're awfully dressed up for dinner at my sister's house, too."

He nodded, but she was going to keep prodding. "I was thinking maybe we should just call her and tell her we're staying home."

He shrugged his shoulder. "If you want to."

"Really? You wouldn't mind staying and watching TV with me?"

"New MythBusters is on. Complete entertainment where I'm concerned."

Arianna looked in the mirror. She widened her eyes and added her mascara to her lashes. John had gone back into the bedroom, and she could hear drawers open and close on the dresser.

Arianna batted her eyes and then looked in the doorway again. There he stood with two flannel shirts.

"Which one do you want me to lounge in? The red or the blue?"

God, he was sexy. And he was all hers.

"I'm almost done, and we'll go to dinner at my sister's house."

"Really? Jamie and Adam are blowing up something big tonight."

Arianna pursed her lips. She'd thought she'd trapped him and he'd tell her that something was going on at Regan's, but he wasn't budging. Maybe she was making it all up. There was no secret party. No one was doing anything for her fortieth birthday.

Guilt squeezed in her belly. They'd done enough, hadn't they? After all, she had her theater, and it was more amazing than she ever thought it could be. If she'd waited to do it on her own, she wouldn't have the Rockwell Theater. She'd have some store front, with only folding chairs for acting lessons.

It had been selfish for her to think they'd do something more. Worse, it was horrible that she'd expected it.

When she turned around, John was wearing his red flannel shirt instead of his button down dress shirt.

"Though I love that shirt, and I think you're extremely sexy in it, put on the other shirt you had. They're waiting on us."

John let out a grunt. "Fine, but you owe me a night on the couch with MythBusters."

"Deal."

"I want pizza and beer."

"Anything."

He pulled the shirt off, walked toward her, and wrapped it around her. "And I want *you* to wear the shirt. Nothing else."

She wrapped her arms around him and pressed her palms against his bare back. "Nothing else?"

"Maybe some thigh-high stockings. But, nothing else."

She slowly nodded her head, and her curls brushed her shoulders. "I'll see what I can do."

Arianna was quiet on the ride to Zach and Regan's. John wondered if she knew about the party. He'd done all he could to discourage any thought.

He wasn't sure what he'd have done if she had put on her sweats and called his bluff to lounge and watch TV.

The ring case dug into his leg. He knew it had been dumb to just put it in his pocket, but as of yet, she hadn't noticed.

He reached for her hand and gave it a squeeze. "Are you okay?"

"Yes. I had a moment back home where I was feeling a bit selfish."

"Why's that?"

She let her shoulders drop and let out a long breath. "I was thinking that we were going out to Regan's house for some big party, and that's why I gussied up and then you were all smokin' in your dressed up clothes."

He grinned. She was flustered, and it was endearing.

Arianna pulled the strap on her seatbelt as though it might be choking her. "I was feeling bad that no one had done anything special for my birthday, and it's just around the corner."

"Tuesday. It's Tuesday."

She laughed. "You're a keeper, Forrester."

"Good."

"But it hit me that I was being selfish. No one should get me a gift or throw me a party. You all sunk everything into the theater. You've all been thinking of me the whole time."

"Still, it's okay to want something special."

"No." She shook her head and set her eyes on him. "It's not okay. How greedy is it to want a party? To want to have dinner with the people I love and celebrate my life."

"It's not greedy."

"It feels that way."

"So what do you want to do about it? Would you, at least, like to have everyone over for birthday cake? Forty is a very exciting age. You're going to be amazing at forty, but then again, you already are."

She chuckled, which meant she was lightening up. "You know, I would love that. Do you mind?"

"For you, anything."

As they drove down the long road that led to her sister's house, she could see the cars of her family. Why did she ever need a party when her family was there?

Arianna had learned to sit in the truck until John opened the door for her. He was old fashioned, and she needed to not be so eager and let him take care of her, just a little bit.

John opened the door and helped her down. She always seemed to land right in his arms. He gave her a soft kiss.

"I know it's not your birthday, but would you like one of your presents anyway?"

She narrowed her eyes on him. She should say no, but she'd always been a sucker for a present. "Whatcha got?"

John smiled, reached past her, and pulled open the glove compartment. He took out an envelope and handed it to her.

Arianna quickly lifted the flap and looked inside—then up at him, speechless.

"You wanted to go on vacation."

"You didn't have to do this because I threw a fit over going somewhere."

He gathered her in his arms again. "I told you all that because I'd already bought the tickets."

"You're too good for me."

"No, but I think we are just right for each other, and we came along at just the right time."

Arianna rested her head against his chest. "Is this why we never made any moves on each other?"

"Maybe it was."

The front door to the house opened, and Curtis stood in the doorway with Avery in his arms. "You know we're waiting dinner on you two. I'm hungry. So stop being selfish and get your butts in here."

Arianna laughed. She had John and her family. What more could she need in life?

John watched Arianna run up the front steps of the house and scoop Avery into her arms. Curtis kissed her on the cheek and then waited for him to walk through the door.

"Everyone is in the back, in the kitchen."

Arianna walked through the house, and John heard the loud "surprise" that was shouted from her family and the many friends they'd had gather there.

Avery stirred in her arms, and she held her protectively closer. She turned her head to look at John and she smiled. They hadn't disappointed her. She was sure they never could.

Simone had quickly taken her daughter back, and Arianna went around the room and gave every guest there a hug and spoke to them as though they were the honored guest. There was something special in the way she could make each person feel as though he, or she, was the only one in the room.

Curtis moved in next to John and handed him a beer. "Did she know?"

"I think she wanted to think it was what was going on, but she couldn't get it out of me."

"She'd have been disappointed if we didn't do this."

John shook his head. "I don't think so. She knows what everyone put into the theater, and it means the world to her."

"She deserves that. I've never known anyone so full of energy and life than my own sister. I know that she will not only make that theater something special, but she'll touch lives. She doesn't know it yet, but she will."

"Like Simone?" John motioned to Curtis's fiancée, who was talking to a guest in the corner.

"She didn't know she had it in her to change lives. But she changed one, and that seemed to be her calling. She's establishing a foundation through the clinic to help people find jobs and receive clothing and food."

He'd heard that, but hearing the excitement in Curtis's voice made it seem bigger than life. "I think she'll do great."

Arianna headed toward them. She moved toward Curtis first and wrapped her arms around him. "I love you. Thank you for helping put this together."

"Simone lives for this. Do you really think I had anything to do with it?"

She gave him a noisy kiss on the cheek. "Yes." Then she turned to John. "And what would you have done if I'd put my sweat pants on and watched TV?"

"I would have had to have sedated you and brought you anyway."

She moved toward him and wrapped her arms around him. "I'm nervous knowing you can keep a secret this well."

"I'll tell you a secret." He smiled, and she rolled her eyes.

"What?"

"I hate keeping secrets. This has been horrible."

"You're good at it."

"Well, let's hope I don't have to keep too many of them. I'd rather be upfront about everything."

"Nicely said, Forrester. So then give me what you have in your pocket."

He chuckled. "I thought I'd had that hidden fairly well."

"Um, no."

John reached into his pocket and touched the box, then pulled his hand out without having grabbed it.

"Can I have everyone's attention?" That was probably the most uncomfortable phrase he'd ever spoken aloud. Had her sister and her sister-in-laws not helped him pick out the ring, he'd have given it to her while they watched MythBusters. That was more their style. But this was going to need some onlookers.

When he looked back at Arianna, her eyes had gone wide. Yeah, he'd taken her by surprise, too.

Regan ran past all the guests. She had her camera in her hand, and he figured if that didn't give it away, nothing would.

John took Arianna's hand. It shook in his.

"I wanted to give you something very special for your birthday."

"You did. You're taking me to San Francisco."

He'd heard Madeline gasp and then sniff back tears. Regan, on the other hand, was doing some kind of dance just behind him.

"I am. But to mark your fortieth year and to seal the commitment you and I have made to each other, I thought you needed something with a bit more longevity."

Tears were forming in her eyes. God, he wished he'd have done this in the privacy of their own home.

He pulled the box from his pocket. Arianna pulled her hand away and clasped them both over her mouth.

John opened the box, and this time he heard Emily Keller begin to cry.

"Arianna, I've never loved anyone as much as I love you. And I know we said no marriage licenses and no wedding vows, but that didn't mean you didn't deserve the most beautiful ring your sisters could pick out for you."

She shuttered and dropped her hands. "You took them shopping with you?"

"If I'd have picked this out, you'd have a Ring Pop."

She laughed through her tears.

John pulled the ring from the box and handed the empty box to Madeline, who was now nearly sobbing.

He pulled Arianna's hand toward him. "I love you. I want you to wear this as a daily celebration of my love for you. That commitment is real. I'm never going anywhere."

He was sure she'd have said something, if she could. Her nose was red, and her breaths came in quick pants. Tears rolled down her cheeks. She was the most beautiful mess he'd ever seen.

"How many more secrets do you have?" She laughed as he slid the ring on her finger.

"Only one more, but you can have it on Tuesday."

He pulled her into his arms and held her tight. Everything felt right.

John had caught her throughout the night looking down at her hand.

"I think she likes it," Simone said as she sat down beside him on the sofa.

"You girls did a good job."

"You did not have to use our suggestion. You get all the credit."

"I wanted it to mean something. I wanted her to know how much I love her."

"Oh, I think she knows." Simone touched his arm. "You are a very thoughtful man, John Forrester. I have always enjoyed that about you."

"Thoughtful? Couldn't say I'd use that word."

"I have seen you with your employees. You are strict, but you have a good heart. You care about them."

He did care about his employees. Every one of them—usually. And if he couldn't make himself care about them then they didn't need to be working for Zach's company.

"I hear you're the caring one. You're starting an organization at the clinic to help people find jobs?"

"I know a lot of people with big businesses. I do not see why I should not help people with what I have." She brushed her hands over her skirt. "I may not have wealth in money anymore to help people, but I have so much more. I wish *I* were my father's riches, as Avery and Curtis are mine."

He never thought he'd see eye to eye with Simone Pierpont, but with that statement, he sure did.

John had never thought himself a wealthy man, not monetarily speaking, but seated next to a woman, once worth perhaps a billion dollars, he thought perhaps they were as wealthy as two people could be.

CHAPTER EIGHTEEN

John had personally watched Arianna shine her ring at least ten times over the weekend. When they'd gone to the grocery store, he noticed how she held the charge slip so everyone could see her finger. It was as if suddenly she was a hand model, and it thrilled him.

Regan had been right. Attaching a proposal to the ring would have been the biggest mistake. They were right where they needed to be—together, in love, and happy.

Monday morning, Arianna had set up meetings with local business owners. She would need their support when the theater opened. She understood networking, and he loved watching her work, but construction called, and he spent his day receiving the shipment of theater seats, which were two weeks early.

Eduardo convinced Carlos to excuse him from school so he could work on Arianna's office. John wasn't sure how much he agreed with that, but if an educator agreed to call in his own son, who was he to judge?

He hadn't seen much of Eduardo all day except at lunch time, out at the break truck, when he'd bought him a Pepsi and a hot dog. Now they were an hour from quitting time, and he figured he'd better make sure the room would be ready for Arianna's surprise tomorrow morning.

When John opened the door to her office, he wasn't sure why he'd even questioned that it might not be done in time or be absolutely brilliant. Eduardo Keller was a natural.

Eduardo was in the corner behind the desk, which would be his aunt's. He was finishing a detail, no doubt.

"Hey, John, what do you think?"

John looked around the room. Every detail was exactly as Eduardo had described it less than a week earlier. The colors were vibrant. There were two desks in one half of the room as well as a large table where they could work. The other side of the room was divided by a wall, which had a window so Arianna could see the door, and had a desk and two chairs. The windows looking out into the street had blinds on them, and there was even a plant in the corner.

"You have certainly showed me your potential. Your uncle will be very proud of you."

"I hope so. Maybe he'll give me a reference into Virginia Tech."

John felt the unmistakable warmth of pride in his chest. "I'm sure he will. And you can expect one from me, too."

Eduardo's head snapped up. He was suppressing his grin. "Really?"

"I know what you're capable of. You and Zach are very alike, you know." He crossed his arms over his chest. "Shows you just how old I am. I remember Zach learning the ropes."

"This is what I want to do."

"And you'll do well. I can't wait to see your aunt's face when she looks at this place."

Eduardo's shoulders dropped. "I wish I could see her expression."

John contemplated for a moment. "Call your dad and tell him I'll bring you home. Let me get your aunt down here."

John walked out into the lobby, which was looking very good if he did think so himself. He pulled his phone from his pocket and dialed Arianna. She had to come down now. Eduardo deserved to see her face.

John had felt bad about disrupting her afternoon. Arianna had just filled a bubble bath and poured a glass of wine, she'd told him. But he promised it would be worth it, *and* that when they got home, he'd join her for the bubble bath and that glass of wine.

That had worked for her, and she was on her way.

By the time she pulled up in front of the theater, the last of the construction crew was pulling away. John smiled as he opened the front door and watched her climb out of her car. The place wasn't so eerie anymore. It didn't have that *inhabited* feel.

He kept the smile on his face even though he was thinking about the night that someone had tried to hurt Arianna and April. It hurt to think that someone would break into the building and deface it after they had put so much work into it.

She hadn't said much more about the phone calls or text messages she'd received, and he knew she would no longer keep them a secret from him. She understood the severity of the situation. But that part still haunted him. Someone had taken a lot of time to mess with her and follow her. All he could hope, as she walked toward him with her hair piled on top of her head and her feet clad in UGG boots, was that her terror was over. It was time for

Arianna to become part of the community again and to do what she wanted to do.

Arianna walked up the steps. "I got a phone call from this location. A man said to meet him here, and he'd make it worth my while."

John laughed when he noticed she had on flannel pajamas under her coat. "I see you dressed up for the occasion."

"Well, only the best for you, dear."

She kissed him softly on the lips, and it warmed him throughout.

He shook his head. "What if I was going to take you out to a fancy dinner?"

She gave him a look over from head to toe. "With an inch of construction dust on your shoes, and what is this?" She reached up to his hair and pulled out a small piece of wire. "Do I have lights?"

He nodded. "Yes, you do."

"So why am I here?"

"Another birthday surprise, but the person in charge of it wanted to be here when you received it."

He stepped back through the door and closed it behind Arianna as soon as she crossed the threshold.

She looked around. "It's starting to look very nice in here, Forrester."

"I aim to please."

"And please you do."

"C'mon." He took her hand.

He led her down the hall toward the office and very calmly led her in, but she gasped and stopped at the door.

"Oh, John! This is wonderful."

He smiled. "I know."

Eduardo moved around the wall and walked toward them. "Do you really like it?"

"It is perfect." She turned to John. "This is my surprise?"

"Yes."

"So who wanted to see my face?"

John pointed to Eduardo.

She turned to look at her nephew. "You did this?"

"Yes."

"You and John?"

John shook his head. "Oh, no. I gave this young man a project. I asked him what he'd see in here and told him he had a week to make it work. I think he did an excellent job."

Arianna moved through the office right to Eduardo and wrapped her arms around his neck. John laughed when he only staggered back, trapped by his aunt's embrace.

"I love it, Ed! You're amazing. Just amazing."

"Thank you," he said, muffled against her.

Arianna pulled back. "Let me see. Creative colors. A window in the wall so I can see the door, but the room is still one room. Two more desks for others to work here. A table to lay my stuff out on. And, is that a closet to store stuff?"

John chuckled, shoved his hands in his pocket, and leaned back on his heels. "Well, Eduardo, I'm very impressed. You did see exactly what she'd want."

She turned back to Eduardo, who had managed to move at least two feet away from her. "That's what you'd told him?"

"Yes."

"I think you've found your calling." She threw her hands in the air. "We need to take him to dinner to celebrate."

"You're in your pajamas," John reminded her.

"And you have construction crap in your hair."

Eduardo cleared his throat. "I skipped school today, and I have a test tomorrow. So I'd better go home and study."

Arianna smiled. "You are your father's child. School first."

Eduardo shrugged.

"Well, we have to celebrate." She thought for a moment. "Ice cream on our way to take you home?"

"Can't turn that down."

Arianna drove home after they had treated Eduardo to ice cream, and she'd convinced John, one more time when they went back to the theater to pick up her car, to go in and look at her office. She couldn't believe how well it fit her, and she couldn't wait to move in and start working. John wasn't going to get rid of her now.

She turned up the radio when she heard the familiar voice of Luke Bryan, and she was in the kind of mood that a good southern twang made her heartbeat kick up a notch. But she knew it was because it reminded her of John. And even though he was only a mile ahead of her, thinking about him made her happy too.

There had been a bit of a sting, knowing she was facing forty. John had greatly eased that. She knew the surprise party was all Regan's doing, but the ring…oh, the ring.

She looked down at her finger. Even in the dark of her car, the sapphire sparkled up at her. Certainly there wasn't a happier forty-year-old in the world.

John was parked in front of the house when she pulled up. That meant he was still looking out for her. She was very sure that the worst was behind them. The theater was nearing completion, and no matter what John said, she was sure it would be done before July.

Every entrance and exit had been rekeyed and redesigned, so no vagrants were going to be keeping house there. The outside was scheduled to be painted the next week, and John had contacted the city to have the lights fixed on the street. But this is how it would be now—forever.

She liked the way it felt, knowing he'd always be protective over her.

He was at her car before she climbed out.

"Hovering, Forrester?"

"Never going to be too careful."

"Remember," she patted her purse, "I'm protected."

He rubbed his cheek, and she could hear the scratch of his whiskers against his hand. "Don't get too confident, okay? My rules still apply, for now. You don't go to the theater unless I'm there."

"Right." She chuckled and shut the car door, but he quickly caught her arm and turned her toward him.

"I'm not kidding, Arianna. You don't go unless I tell you to be there. I'm not messing around with this. Whoever was calling you and following you is still out there."

His grip had become tight, though she knew he didn't mean to hurt her. "Okay. Okay. I promise not to come down unless you tell me to."

He let go of her and even took a step back. Obviously he realized how tight he'd been holding her.

She gave a nod toward the house. "C'mon, worry wart, you owe me a bubble bath."

Lavender had eased her mind. Bubbles had added to the ambiance of the moment. Leaning up against John in the warm water had been the relaxation she'd been looking for hours earlier. Only now, she had the knowledge of her surprise, and in her mind, she was making a list of all the things she'd be taking to *her* office tomorrow.

"Now that we are getting closer to having the theater finished, I suppose I should make sure my business licenses are in order and the sales tax license, too."

John moved her hair from her shoulder and drizzled water over her neck. "Sales tax? You have to have sales tax for a play ticket?"

She laughed. "You nearly pay sales tax for anything anymore. There is even tax on the Junior Mints."

"And yet I had to call the city and tell them three of the street lights in front of the theater were out. Nice."

She leaned in against him. "And I thank you very much."

"You know, when the theater is all done, I have to go back to building other buildings. My time with you will be over."

"Just our time *working*. Our time will never be over."

He lifted her hand out of the water, and her sapphire dripped with soap. "You didn't take this off?"

"You don't take off a wedding ring. So I didn't see any reason to take it off."

John gave a low hum which resonated through his chest and against her back. "I guess the only part about not being married is that you'll never have my last name."

Arianna considered it. That was always one of the reasons to never get married. Giving up her identity wasn't part of her game plan. But there would be some great pride in being a Forrester.

"You're right." She wiggled her toes in the water. "Arianna Forrester. It doesn't sound bad, does it?"

"I rather like it." He brushed his hands down her arms and back up. "Arianna Keller-Forrester."

"That's not bad either."

"Of course, there is nothing wrong with Arianna Keller."

She sighed as she turned her head to look up at him. "No, there isn't anything wrong with that either."

"You're getting sentimental in your old age." He touched her face. "I was waiting for a fight when I made that comment about my last name."

Arianna rested her head against his shoulder and interlaced their fingers. "I know, it's just…"

"Not what you've ever wanted."

"There was never a right last name before."

This time John shifted to look at her. "And you're saying that I have the right last name?"

She chuckled. "It's not just the name. It's you."

"I tell you what. Let's make a pact, and we can sign it in bubbles." He grinned. "If ever you change your mind about wanting one of those pieces of paper which states that we have made a commitment to each other, and you'd rather have the name Forrester or even Keller-Forrester, I will never argue."

Arianna pursed her lips. "Is that a marriage proposal?"

"It's a proposal to accept a proposal, should you need a proposal. Or something like that."

She turned around and straddled him, sending water over the sides of the tub. "I'm not going to marry you."

"And I'm not going to ask."

"But I really do like that name of yours."

"It's yours for the keeping."

"I'll think about it."

"You do that. And while you're thinking about it, you'd better get some towels and clean this up. If it gets under the tile…"

"You'll fix it."

That comment had him moving swiftly and dunking her into the tub.

She was in love. Even as she spit bubbles from her mouth, she was contemplating the name Arianna Forrester.

CHAPTER NINETEEN

Arianna hadn't anticipated that John wouldn't be at the theater when she arrived the next morning with a box full of personal belongings for her new office.

He hadn't told her to come and she was earlier than usual, and now she knew she was in trouble.

She greeted the site workers as she passed them on her way to her office. Her arms were loaded down with a big box and her Starbucks. Finally, as she reached her office door, one of the plumbers ran to her aid.

"You look like you're ready to do some business," he said with his slow Tennessee drawl. She'd missed home.

"I am ready." She pushed open the door, and the man followed her to her desk and set down the box.

"My wife wanted me to mention that she's a pianist. She'd be awfully excited to come help you out if you could use her. She plays for the church choir every Sunday."

"I think that sounds wonderful." Arianna turned and pulled a pen from a cup in the box he'd sat on the desk. She fished around for her notebook, too. "Here. Will you write down her name and phone number?"

"Sure. You gonna call her?"

"I think I might if she's really interested. I have a show already in the works."

"Neat." The man went about writing down the information. "Thanks. I'll let her know I talked to you."

"And thank you for the help."

"My pleasure." He gave her a little wave and walked out of the office.

"Are you holding meetings with the plumbers already?" John's voice resonated through the room.

"He helped me in."

"You don't usually get here this early." There was a crease between his brows. She knew he was trying not to sound as angry as he was.

"I was just excited to move a few things in. I know the building isn't done yet, but I have things in motion already. I should get to work, right?"

He walked toward her, placed a small kiss on her lips, and stepped back. "I'm not going to keep you from being here, I suppose."

"John, everything is okay. You're going to have to trust me to be down here alone at some point."

He nodded. "I still don't like it. You have your gun?"

"Yes."

"Loaded?"

"Always."

He let out a deep breath. "I have some things to tend to. I assume I'll find you here?"

She smiled. "I have pictures to set up on my new bookcases. I have files already full of notes. I even brought some old scripts and sheet music to put in my closet."

He gave her a chuckle and finally a smile formed on his lips. "You're happy."

"Don't ever remember being happier."

With a nod he was gone, and she was alone in her very special part of the world that Eduardo designed for her.

By noon she had a list of things that needed to be added to the room. She needed a fax machine, a printer/scanner, and a coffee pot. She'd seen John's coffee pot in the trailer out back. It looked as though it were always full because of the grime of coffee on the inside of the pot.

Over the past few months she could say she knew him well enough to assume he'd say if it were cleaned it would ruin the taste of the coffee. However, having seen how he lived, she was surprised anything he owned was that dirty. Job site mentality, she decided.

She was on the phone with the company she would acquire the rights to produce *Annie* when John walked into the office with a burrito wrapped in tinfoil.

She motioned to him to set it on the table. He did so and then wandered around the office.

Arianna turned off her phone when she was finished with the call and looked up at him. "How is it you don't weigh four hundred pounds eating those burritos everyday?"

"I never stop moving. I burn them off."

"Well, I need to schedule some dance classes in this place soon so I can start to work mine off. I've see the way you look at me when I eat. It makes me nervous that it gives you such pleasure."

He only smiled as he peeled back the foil on his lunch.

"Looks like you're right at home here."

"Getting there."

"Ed said you'd need a table to spread out on. He said that's what you'd do."

She tucked her lips between her teeth to keep from smiling. She'd been pegged by a fifteen-year-old.

"I need to see what I'm doing. I'm a visual person."

"And very appealing to my visual."

"It's a good thing you won't be hanging around here much longer. I don't know how I'd get any work done."

He bit into his burrito. "When will you be done today?"

"I don't know. I'm just plugging away. Why?"

"I think I'll be late. I want to get a few more of these jobs done before next week. I want everything nearly complete before we leave for San Francisco."

He took another bite and she watched him enjoy the homemade burrito. She on the other hand didn't have an appetite for it.

"Maybe we should move our trip. Until everything here is running smooth."

He nodded slowly. "Don't want to go?"

"No, I didn't say that. There is just a lot to do here."

"Honey, there always will be." He finished the burrito and wadded up the tinfoil. "I'm sure that even when this place is fully operational I'll be spending my evenings here either popping popcorn, taking tickets, or building some set. As long as I'm with you everything will be perfect." He stood and looked down at her. "Besides, I haven't had a vacation in four years. I think I'm due."

Arianna let out a sigh. "You're right. So do you think anyone has ever been caught having sex on Alcatraz?"

That put some color in his cheeks and he was belly laughing by the time he rounded the desk to kiss her. "Younger women have some kinky ideas, don't they?"

"Only to see if they can make their old men blush."

He gave a grunt and a nod and left her alone in her office.

Arianna worked until five o'clock. It wasn't until then that she realized the entire front of the theater had been deserted for hours.

The sun was still out, not that spring was pushing through, but there was a chill in the old building. It wasn't enough to put on her heavy coat, but she'd want to bring a jacket and leave it in the office. Oh, and she should buy a coat rack too. She made a mental note as she walked out into the lobby.

The concession area looked almost ready for business, but she knew that was deceiving. She looked around. No one was there, but she didn't feel alone.

"Is anyone here?"

There was no answer.

It was her imagination getting the best of her. Someone was probably working down the hall. She walked further toward the concession stand. The glass was dusty and the shelves had been left to be stained, but right in front of her was a business card, face down.

Arianna picked it up and turned it over.

PIERPONT OIL
PARIS, FRANCE

She looked around again. Who would have left that there? Surely John or Zach had it in their hand as they'd walked through the lobby at some point.

Arianna tucked it into her pocket and headed toward the theater to find John.

The theater was beginning to look beautiful again. The sconces had been rewired and walls had been painted a beautiful golden color. As she walked toward the stage she realized the floor had been repaired and it was obviously ready for the chairs and red carpet.

A few men were working in the cat walk, repairing the beams. Lights flickered up in the light booth. Someone was wiring the switches up there too. It wouldn't be long and there would be performers on the stage and patrons in the seats and she'd be behind stage lapping it up. Who would ever have thought that she would own the theater and not just dream about being in one?

John was on his phone when she opened the trailer door and walked in. He'd narrowed his eyes at her as cold air blew in, but when he'd seen it was her, his face softened, but only slightly. There was something wrong and she could tell by the way he held his body and tapped his pen on the desk.

Arianna walked to the far side of the trailer where there was a table, much like her table in her office, only this one was covered with blue prints of the theater and lists of jobs that still needed to be done.

John obviously knew the time frame for completion of the theater better than she had. She thought it looked almost done, but the number of items to be done on the list were many. Obviously, she didn't know much at all.

She tried not to listen to the conversation he was having, that wasn't part of her business, but his voice was raising and guilt was plaguing her—she should have stayed inside until he'd come for her.

A moment later he turned off his phone and let out a grunt. She figured that was prime opportunity for her to acknowledge him.

"Something wrong?" She had to ask the obvious.

"Inspection on the other build just failed. There is nothing we've done different than on any other building, but this certain inspector has a stick up his ass over Tyler Benson."

"My nephew Tyler Benson?"

John let his shoulders drop and shook his head. "Of course not. Your nephew's grandfather."

"Who has been gone nearly five years?"

"Yes."

Arianna could imagine his frustration. She walked around the desk, leaned up against it, and pulled John in front of her.

"I don't think I ever met the man, but from what I've heard he was a very kind and generous man."

John brushed her hair from her face and looked down at her. "He was. That's why people like this make me so mad. But it's a personal vendetta. Tyler fired his brother, so now he red flags us."

"Is that even legal?"

"Oh, he's straight up. Most inspectors would give you some time to fix things they find. This one wants to just close you down." He rested his hands on her shoulders. "I'm going to have to head over there."

"Will you be long?"

"Probably. Don't wait up."

She forgot words like those existed in relationships. Then again the last relationship she'd had, in which they were spoken, had been said when Eric was home with his wife.

There was hurt there and she didn't realize it until John had muttered the same phrase. This time, however, she knew he was off to a job site and when the job had been fixed he'd be home to her.

"Maybe I'll see if my sister can get away and we can steel away the other two and go out for a girls' night."

This time he laughed. "You think you can steel away three mothers from their families?"

Arianna smiled. "I think I can."

But even as she said it she began to wonder. After all she was the only one without responsibilities to anyone other than herself.

As John began to gather his paperwork she sucked in a breath. That was what she wanted, a life free of the complications of building a family. It would work out perfect in the long run.

Theater ran late into the night and sometimes early into the morning. John's job called for him to start early and obviously the job didn't always end at five.

They were going to be perfect for each other in this relationship. But she really wanted some time with her sisters and now that he'd brought it up, she wondered if they'd be able to drop everything just to spend time with her.

CHAPTER TWENTY

It had taken some finagling, but Arianna was seated at Olive Garden waiting for her sisters to arrive.

Madeline had walked through the door first.

Arianna hadn't noticed how much her hair had grown back in a year. It was still very short and lighter than it had been before. But for the first time in a very long time, Madeline didn't wear a wig or a scarf.

She hurried over to Arianna and kissed her on the cheek. Her skin was cold, and it gave Arianna a chill.

"I'm so glad you called." Madeline pulled her coat off and set it on the back of her chair. "I've been craving breadsticks."

Arianna pushed the basket toward her, and immediately Madeline bit into one.

"Yep, that's what I wanted."

Arianna laughed. "Thanks for coming."

"Are you kidding me? I have missed our impromptu dinners. Besides, Carlos is grading exams. He's not the nicest person when he's doing that."

"Oh, I've seen the wrath." Arianna took a breadstick too, and then noticed Simone and Regan both had walked through the door, each carrying an infant seat covered in a blanket.

Arianna stood from her seat as they headed toward her.

Regan's eyebrows were drawn together. "What's wrong? Why did you have to meet us?"

Arianna's heart sunk right into the pit of her stomach. "I'm sorry. I just wanted to be with all of you."

"I thought something had happened to you."

"No. I missed my sisters and John had to work late..."

"So I'm being ungrateful and paranoid?"

Arianna wrapped her arms around her sister and held her tight. With all that was going on in her life, she hadn't been too panicked about things, but obviously her sister had—with good reason.

She took her nephew's seat from her sister and sat down, balancing the seat on her lap. Slowly she removed the blanket that had been draped over the carrier and peered down at Spencer, all bundled up and sleeping.

Could anything be more precious?

Then she looked up at Simone who had pulled a very alert Avery from her seat. She was dressed in a little pink dress with pink tights and a matching headband.

Arianna felt the sting of tears in her eyes, and she went about setting Spencer down between her and Regan and then walking around the table to reach for Avery.

Simone looked up at her as she picked up her niece. "Why are you crying?"

"I don't know. I guess I'm just a little emotional."

Avery's eyes tried to focus on her and a small smile formed on her lips. That was what it was all about—the love of her sisters and their children. Oh, this sweet, little angel was going to be as spoiled as the others. Arianna felt it burning in her to give her anything she'd ever need.

She walked back around the table and sat down with Avery in her arms.

Madeline reached for another breadstick. "So, are you getting excited for your trip?"

"Trip? Oh, San Francisco? Yes, I think it will be good for us to have some alone time."

"A honeymoon, in a way?"

Arianna hadn't really thought about that, but she supposed it was. After all, she had the ring and the man. "Maybe. I told him we should have sex on Alcatraz."

Simone's eyes shot open wide, Regan shook her head, and Madeline busted out laughing and had to cover her mouth to keep the bite she'd taken from falling out.

Regan readjusted the blanket at Spencer's feet. "I can't believe you said that."

"Yes you can. C'mon, you're getting soft on me."

"Motherhood will do that to you."

Arianna could see that. Madeline was a bit more free. Her brush with death and the fact that her children were older allowed her to not be so uptight. Regan and Simone, on the other hand, were a bit more ridged.

Avery watched Arianna as she fussed with her dress. "Simone, how are plans going for your new business?"

"It is not a business, really. More of an organization to help." She sipped her water. "It is going well. We are still in the planning stages, but I am very proud of it. In fact…" She stopped and picked up her purse. After searching, she pulled out three business cards and handed them to everyone.

"A Better Day. That is the name of your organization?"

"Yes."

"I like it." Arianna ran her finger across the raised print. "You know, maybe we can mix my grand opening with your organization. We can fundraise for you and build a community for me. Who knows, by then I might even have some job openings."

Simone's eyes lit up, though she remained poised. "I think that would be wonderful."

Madeline held up the card. "This card reads Simone Keller."

Simone smiled. "Pierpont no longer holds any value for me. The connections that I have, and those I will make, will know me as a Keller, so I thought it appropriate."

Arianna felt those tears again. Keller. It was a name of pride, and it was hers. And if someone like Simone Pierpont wanted to give up a name that meant prestige and wealth all over the world in order to take on the name Keller, Arianna knew for sure she didn't want to ever give it up.

The evening had been just what Arianna had needed. A night with the women she loved, and Simone fit right into their group.

She thought it was wonderful to hear Madeline talk about Clara's excitement about performing with her aunt. And when Arianna had told her about the office Eduardo had built for her, Madeline had broken down into tears.

Arianna had also been filled in on just how good Christian was at baseball. College scouts were already looking at him, and he had years of high school left.

It floored her that any of their children would be athletic. She knew Zach ran, but really, that was the extent of athleticism in the family. Christian was changing that. Madeline said his dream was to go pro, and from the sounds of it, he'd make it.

The rest of the night had been spent cuddling her niece and nephew and trying to get Simone to spill wedding plans. They'd had no luck. Simone and Curtis were planning a secret elopement with a big party after. Not one detail had been dropped.

The house was still dark when she pulled into the driveway. It was almost nine-thirty. She was sure John would have been home already.

Arianna parked the car and walked up to the door. She slipped the key into the lock and the door pushed open.

How could she have forgotten to lock the door?

She closed the door and locked it behind her and then proceeded to turn on the lamp in the living room. There was a moment when she decided her mind must be slipping. The house was freezing. Had she forgotten to turn the heat up, too?

Arianna walked through to the kitchen and turned on the light.

Her heart began racing when she noticed the back door wide open.

"John! John!" Her voice shook. She was frantic and frozen in place.

Someone had broken into the house. What if someone was still there?

She heard noise in the basement—in John's place.

Arianna took a breath to yell for him again, but her voice had stilled in her throat. She heard footsteps on the stairs.

With the only moment of clarity she'd had, she realized her purse was still on her shoulder.

She patted the side of it and could feel the shape of the gun. Slowly she unlatched the hook and pulled the gun from her purse.

She shook as she gripped the gun. Her feet planted firmly, she took aim at the basement door as the footsteps grew closer.

As the person in the basement neared the top of the stairs, she swallowed hard and cocked the gun.

"Arianna? Are you home? The heater is…" John stopped in the doorway and looked at her standing there with the gun pointed right at his head.

Her body shook until she thought the gun might fall from her hands. John walked slowly to her, and tears began to pour down her cheeks.

"Sweetheart," he said softly as he walked slowly toward her. "Put the gun down."

She lowered it to her side.

John took it from her hand carefully and uncocked the gun. He set it on the counter and pulled her into his arms.

"Honey, you're shaking like a leaf. Calm down."

"The door. The house was…"

"Shh." He smoothed a hand over her hair. "The furnace went out. I'm trying to fix it. I had the door open so I could go out to my truck."

"I thought…" She couldn't even get the words out.

John let go of her long enough to shut the door. Then he guided Arianna to the living room and set her on the couch. He reached for a throw and wrapped it around her shoulders.

"Calm down." John sat down next to her and put his arm around her.

Arianna sucked in a deep breath and let it out very slow. Then, she did it again.

John was keeping her very close. It was comforting. But the moment that the thought was clear—she could have killed John—the tears were back.

"What if I'd shot you?"

"You didn't."

"I was going to." She sucked back a sob. "I could have killed you."

"You were prepared."

"The front door wasn't locked. And then the back door was wide open and…"

John pushed back. "The front door wasn't locked?" Arianna shook her head, and John stood. "I didn't go through the front door."

Arianna covered her mouth with her hand as John moved to the door.

He opened it and looked at the lock. "It isn't jimmied. No one has messed with the door or the lock."

"So maybe I just left it unlocked?"

"I think so." He closed the door and locked it again.

How could she have been so forgetful? In all her life she'd never left the front door unlocked. Maybe she'd been too excited to have dinner with the girls. That had to be it.

"Listen. I have to get that furnace working. It is freezing in here. Go upstairs. Run yourself a hot bath and get yourself calm."

Arianna nodded.

John kissed her gently and headed back to the basement.

With the blanket still around her shoulders, Arianna walked out to the kitchen and picked up her purse and the gun. She slid the gun back into the pocket of the purse and headed upstairs.

As she walked back through the kitchen, she looked down at the table. Simone's business card looked back up at her.

She must have dropped the card on the table when she pulled the gun from her purse.

She walked back through the living room and up to the bathroom. Hopefully the hot water heater was still working, or a hot bath wasn't going to soothe anything.

John had heard the bathtub running, and a moment later, he had the furnace kicking to life. He was glad. If he didn't get the heat going soon, they were going to have to find a motel for the night. He'd been tired and irritated from his findings at the site, but nearly being killed by the woman he loved had him a little jumpy.

Why did she think it was necessary to pull her gun on him? Didn't she say, just the other day, that she thought the worst was behind them, and no one was after her?

Well, something had her scared enough to nearly kill him.

He packed up his tools and thought he shouldn't look at it that way. Yes, he could have been shot, but he hadn't been. Arianna was prepared and cautious, that was all.

By the time he'd made it upstairs, Arianna had tucked herself into bed, bundled in sweat pants, socks and a flannel shirt.

"You don't have that gun tucked up under there with you, do ya?" He smiled, but there were still tears in her eyes.

"I'm very sorry." She wiped her eyes. "What if I'd shot you?"

"Let's just hope you don't have a great shot."

"I have four first place trophies for trap shooting, of course Regan has six."

John unbuttoned his shirt. "Great. She *and* her sister can hit moving targets."

Arianna sat up and looked at him. "I don't remember not locking the door. I've never left a house without locking the door."

John sat down on the bed next to her. "Do you think someone was in the house?"

"I don't know. Nothing is missing. The door isn't broken. It had to have been me."

He took her hands in his. "I'll tell you what. Tomorrow we will look into a security system. Would that make you feel better?"

She leaned in to him and rested her head on his shoulder. "Yes, but what if he is still out there? What if he's not in Paris."

"He's not going to touch you."

"What if he gets to me or Regan? Those boys can't lose their mother."

The sobs were shaking her body, and he pulled her in closer. "Don't think like that. This family is stronger than one man."

As he held her close to him, her breath began to slow.

He'd protect her and her family with his life, if it came down to it. No one would hurt the Keller family. No one.

CHAPTER TWENTY-ONE

John stayed home with Arianna the next day, and just as he'd promised, there was a crew there installing a security system.

Regan had called her four times before lunch to check on her, and Arianna could hear it in her voice. She, too, was scared and now locked in her own house.

This was no way of life.

The bastard couldn't just keep them living in fear, but he was. It had been four years, and he'd been the one to try and kill Regan. Why now was it so important to try and hurt them all?

Of course there still was an obvious issue. Alexander Hamilton was apparently in Paris, and what if it was Eric who was terrorizing her? Then again, what if it was all her imagination?

It was nearly three in the afternoon when the security system had been installed, and John was antsy.

"You can go in to work if you need to," she said as he poured water into the coffee pot for the third time that day.

"I told you I'd stay with you."

"C'mon, I don't want to be away from the theater just because I'm paranoid. I'll go into my office for a few hours, and you can get some work done, too."

He filled the filter with coffee and pushed the brew button. "Are you sure?"

"Yes."

She needed to stay busy, or she knew just contemplating things would make her crazy.

John didn't like Arianna being in her office when he had to be in his, out back of the theater. Too many people came and went out the building for him to keep track of.

But, for a moment, the thought of her standing there pointing a gun at him humored him. He wasn't sure why he was worried about her. He should be worried about himself and his own safety within their house.

He spent an hour checking in with the crews and making sure they were on task. With his clipboard full of notes, he headed back to his office and sat down at his desk.

He looked over the pile of papers and contracts. Surely he'd left them in better order than they were. It was almost as if they'd fallen on the floor, and someone picked them up and threw them on the desk.

Now he was paranoid.

He gathered the papers and stacked them into a neat pile. But at the bottom of the pile, flat on the desk, was a Benson, Benson, and Hart business card.

REGAN KELLER
EXECUTIVE ASSISTANT

John picked up the card and looked it over. How long had that been floating around his desk? Zach had fired Regan four years ago as his assistant.

He tucked the card into his pocket and went back to work.

They had agreed to head home at five, but when John looked down at his watch, it was already past six. He hadn't seen Arianna in hours, and he didn't like that at all.

He cleared off his desk, put on his coat, and locked up the trailer.

The stage lights were on when he walked through the back door, and he could hear music. He was very pleasantly surprised to find Arianna on the stage, dancing and writing down notes.

The crews had gone home. She was alone, and she was happy doing what she was doing. That was what he'd wanted to see. That was the whole reason for this theater.

She'd caught sight of him and smiled, but she didn't stop what she was doing. There was a comfort about her when she was working. He liked how happiness looked on her.

When she was done, she turned off her iPod and looked at him.

John walked toward her. "What are you working on?"

"A dance number for Clara for the grand opening."

"So what was that you were doing?"

"Blocking out a dance number."

He nodded. "Those are your blueprints?"

She laughed. "Yes, I guess they are."

John moved in closer until he was right next to her. He wrapped his arm around her waist, took her hand in his, and pulled her close until their bodies were pressed together. "It's been nearly a year since we last danced together."

"You're right."

John moved her from side to side and then spun her around. "You were lucky I didn't have two left feet. I've seen your brothers dance."

She laughed again, and this time she let her head fall back and the dark curls swung at her shoulders.

"I used to dance on my daddy's feet. And my brothers used to dance on mine."

"I like the thought that we will dance together forever."

Arianna leaned into him and wrapped her arms around his neck. "I love you, Forrester."

"I love you, Keller."

"I never knew I could be so happy."

"Oh, darling, my goal is to make you happy for the rest of your life."

He moved in to kiss her. As their lips touched, the lights above them sparked and flickered. Then the theater was dark.

Arianna clung to him tighter.

He kissed her forehead. "It's okay. Just a lighting issue."

"I'm tired of those little issues that nearly give me heart attacks."

"I'll have them look into it in the morning. Let's go close up your office. I'll turn the power off to the lights, and we'll get home."

John had walked her to her office and then gone back to the booth to make sure the switches were all off. She gathered her notebook and the few sheets of music she had laid out and put them into her bag. As she flung the bag over her shoulder, she noticed that on the corner of her desk was another business card.

CURTIS KELLER
ATTENDING SURGEON

Arianna smiled and pulled her cell phone from her pocket and dialed her brother's number.

"Hey," he said as he answered the phone. She could hear Avery in the background crying.

"I found your card. When did you drop by?"

"What?"

"Your business card was on my desk. I thought I missed you."

"Business card? The only place I have business cards is at the hospital. I think you've lost your mind."

Arianna swallowed hard. She was very sure she was losing her mind.

"So you weren't here?"

"No. Listen, I have to get little miss fussy pants changed. Are you okay?"

She gripped the phone tighter. "Yeah, I'm fine. I probably just dropped the card, and it just surfaced. I love you. Goodnight."

She tucked the card into her pocket and headed out to the lobby where John was just turning off the last of the lights.

"I guess we should get some dinner on the way home," he mentioned as they both walked out the front door of the theater.

"I'm not very hungry. Maybe we can just eat something light at home."

He nodded as he locked the door. "Sensible. That's why I love you."

"I didn't know that was a qualifying quality."

"Honey, there isn't anything you do that doesn't qualify for a reason to love you."

The man was honest, and she liked that. He was comfortable around her, her family, and with himself. What wasn't to love? Even better, he loved her no matter her short comings, and the more scared she was becoming, the more short comings she felt she had.

John parked his truck out back. He realized that the backyard was always dark. They'd need to put a motion light back there. Why have a security system if the lighting sucked?

He noticed Arianna was staring at him as he sat in the truck.

"Everything okay?" she asked as she laid her hand atop his.

"Yeah, sorry. I was just thinking of adding some lights back here."

"I thought we had one."

He gave it some thought. Perhaps they did. He didn't remember it always being so dark. Maybe the bulb had just burnt out.

Now he knew he, too, was frazzled. Little details like that didn't just slip his mind.

He climbed out of the truck and walked around front of it as Arianna climbed out and slammed the door. He took her hand, and they walked up the back steps of the house.

As he slid the key into the door, he looked up at the porch light next to the door. The bulb wasn't burnt out. It was missing. He pushed open the door and entered the code into the new alarm pad. Arianna turned on the kitchen light and went about hanging up her coat.

She was at ease at home. He wasn't going to mention that the bulb was missing from the light. He'd just put in a new one, and everything would be good.

They'd forged dinner from the kitchen, watched a little TV in bed, and now Arianna slept soundly next to him. But John couldn't sleep.

His mind was racing with all the strange things that had been happening around them, but none of them harmful.

Who had been in the theater that night? He knew it was a vagrant, who now was more homeless than before since they'd begun to renovate. But it bothered him that from time to time Arianna would have to deal with that.

The red flags at the build site he'd had to attend to the other day were stupid little things his men never would have missed. It was as though certain items had been removed from the site to make it look as though they'd just been neglected. If it had been malicious, it would have to have been someone familiar with the building or with construction; more than likely someone who had been fired from the build. Hell, that wouldn't be the first angry ex-employee story John had to tell. Then again, nothing was as horrible as the man who attacked Regan after he'd fired him. John would live with that guilt the rest of his life.

But what if it was more?

Who had taken the bulb out of the light out back?

And did Arianna really leave the door unlocked the other day?

He was beginning to think things weren't as quiet as they'd thought they were.

CHAPTER TWENTY-TWO

John had felt guilty letting Arianna sleep and not bringing her with him to work. She had lots to do, but she was exhausted.

He'd set the alarm before he left the house. He'd left her a note on the table. Within a few hours, she'd be by his side, and he'd be more at ease.

When he pulled up to the theater, all of his men were standing out back. They should have been working, and now that had him angry.

"What's going on?" He jumped from his truck and searched the small crowd for Paul, who was in charge of getting them started every morning.

"Doors are locked, and we can't get in," Paul said as he moved from the crowd.

"Key is in the lockbox."

"Lockbox is gone."

John didn't like that at all.

He moved through the crowd and to the door. Sure enough, the box was missing and that meant the key was too.

John fished for his keys from his pocket, unlocked the door, and sent the men in to get their work done. He sought out the man in the group who could rekey the locks and set him to work changing every lock in the place.

There would be no more lockboxes. John would just have to be on site before everyone—always.

Arianna arrived just after eight with her signature Starbucks cup in her hand and her bag of ideas on her shoulder. He'd never been happier to see anyone in his life.

He walked through the lobby and followed her into her office where he shut the door and quickly pulled her into his arms.

She let out a grunt as his body slammed against hers, and then a moan when he took her under with a kiss meant for the bedroom.

"Good morning, Forrester." She smiled up at him. "Remind me to never let you hire women."

"Why's that?"

"If you greet them every morning like this, I'll have a problem with that."

He held her to him even tighter. "I'll never kiss another woman like that again."

"Good to hear." She tilted her head back, and he knew she saw worry in his eyes. "Something's got you all worked up this morning already."

She moved out of his arms and put her belongings on her desk.

"Someone broke off the lockbox and stole the key. The guys were locked out this morning."

"You think someone broke in here?" She began to look around the room.

"No. I can't find any evidence that someone tampered with anything. Just a jokester, I suppose."

She nodded and began unloading her bag. "Why didn't you leave the alarm on at the house this morning?"

John swiftly moved to her. "I did."

"It wasn't on." She reached into her pocket and pulled out a card. "You left this on the table, too."

He looked down at the business card.

ZACH BENSON
CEO

"I didn't leave this."

"It's not mine. I've never had one of his cards. I picked it up because I thought it was Simone's, but the one she gave me was still in my purse."

John turned the card over and looked at the back. The word NEXT was printed on it.

He swallowed hard. "Do you have a lot of work to do today?"

"Yes, why?"

"I just want to know you'll be close."

She nodded. "I hope you don't mind, I'd like to work on the stage again."

He didn't mind that at all. That would keep her even closer.

John hurried out of her office and back to his desk. He sorted through the desk and found Regan's card, which he'd discovered last night. He turned it over.

DIE

He fell into his chair. His heart raced, and his palms had grown damp. Son-of-a-bitch was playing games with them.

John headed back to Arianna's office. She was on the phone, and he waited.

"Okay, I'll see you in just a little bit," she said as she turned off her phone.

"You're leaving? Where are you going?"

Arianna narrowed her stare at him. "You're sure jumpy today. I'm going out to Regan's."

He nodded. Perhaps that was best. They'd be together, and he could head over to Zach's and they could make a plan.

She was watching him again. "Is everything okay with you?" she asked as she stood and walked around her desk.

"Yeah. Bad morning."

"I guess it is. You're dropping things this morning, too." She turned and handed him yet another business card. "I found this on my floor."

She handed him the card.

MADELINE KELLER
LOAN OFFICER

"Were you going to buy a new truck?" She was teasing, but her smile disappeared when he turned the card over.

Again the word NEXT was written on the back.

"What does that mean?" she asked.

"Listen, you get to your sister's, and you just stay there until I call you. Got it?"

"Yeah. John, you're scaring me."

He turned to leave. "Someone is playing games here, and I've about had it."

Arianna drove out to Regan's place, but the good mood she'd been in was slipping. Why had John been so upset?

Regan answered the door when Arianna rang the bell, but she could hear Spencer crying in the other room. Regan flung the door open and was off and running through the house.

"Is he okay?" Arianna shut the door and followed her.

"He's hungry. I think he's getting a cold, and his mother is a bit frazzled."

"Why is that?"

Regan scooped up Spencer and then pointed across the room. Red crayon covered the white wall in big circles.

Arianna tucked her lips between her teeth to keep the smile from forming or the laughter from erupting.

"And where is Van Gough?"

"In his room."

"May I?"

"Yes, but if you promise him anything, I'll kill you."

"Would I do something like that?" Now the smile formed on her lips, and her sister's eyes narrowed. "I'll just go talk to him. You feed the baby and calm down."

She started up the stairs. "It's a good thing I'm here. What would you do without me?"

She could hear Tyler in his room, and she opened the door slowly. "Hey, big guy." He ran right to her, and she scooped him up. She sat down in the big chair in the corner and held him tightly to her. "Did you color on Mommy's walls?"

Tyler shook his head.

"It wasn't you?"

He shook his head again.

"Hmmm. Is mommy paying too much attention to Spencer?"

He didn't answer, but Tyler lifted his head and looked at her.

"Do you think she's forgetting to play with you?"

This time he nodded his head, and Arianna pulled him in tightly.

"You and I have a lot in common, kiddo. Your mommy is my little sister. And sometimes my mom had to take care of her, and she forgot to play with me."

Tyler held her tight, and she thought she might cry if she didn't continue talking. "I had an auntie who would come over and play with me when my little sister and my little brother were born. That way I didn't get bored."

Tyler sat back and looked at her.

Arianna kissed him on the nose. "Would you like to play?"

He crawled out of her lap, took her hand, and led her to the Thomas the Tank Engine set on the floor. This was where she would spend the next hour until Tyler finally fell asleep on the floor, and she then laid him in his bed and covered him with a blanket she remembered Regan having as a child.

When Arianna made it downstairs, Regan was asleep on the couch, and Spencer was asleep in the bassinette next to her. She didn't know just being home with two little kids could wear out an adult, but Regan was proof that it was harder than it sounded.

Arianna went about finding supplies to clean off the wall. Once the crayon had been removed, she started picking up the kitchen and washing dishes.

Poor Regan. Perhaps, she thought, she should forget the theater until all the kids were grown, and she should just help her sisters every day. If Regan was as much a wreck as she looked to be, Arianna couldn't even imagine how Simone was holding up.

Another hour had passed, and Arianna had brewed a pot of coffee. She heard Spencer stirring in the bassinette, so she picked him up. Tyler had woken up, and she'd gone to get him, too.

They'd agreed to do some coloring, in a coloring book, and sat down at the table.

Finally, Regan stumbled into the kitchen.

"I guess I was tired."

"Like I said, what would you do without me?"

Regan wiped her eyes, but Arianna was sure she was wiping away tears. "I don't know. Thank you for coming out."

"My pleasure. Besides John is all worked up over something. I'm better off here."

Regan kissed Tyler on the head and sat down at the table. "How are things going at the theater?"

"Good, but I guess someone stole the lock box and that had set him off."

"Zach said someone sabotaged the other build site, too."

Arianna pursed her lips. John hadn't mentioned that.

Perhaps that was what he'd been talking about, someone playing games. No wonder he wasn't in a very good mood.

John had headed straight over to Zach's office, but one thing he should have learned over the years is that you call first. Zach had taken the day to fly to Oklahoma to survey a new build site. He no longer took long extended trips, only day trips.

Mary Ellen looked up at him from her desk. "Do you want me to get him on the phone?"

"No. I'll talk to him when he gets back. It can all wait until tomorrow."

"Everything on track at the theater?"

He rubbed his chin. He'd forgotten to shave. "It'll be done on time. I'm sure if I get it done early, she'll already have a show ready to put on, too."

"I think it is wonderful what you all did for Arianna."

Just the mention of her name made him happy. "She'll make it great. Just let Zach know I was here if he calls."

John then headed to the other build site to see if things were still on track to get those fixes done. Arianna had texted and said she was still at Regan's and would be staying to help with dinner. He figured that would give him a few hours to see to everything.

By the time he'd checked out the area that had been red flagged, it was five-thirty. The crew had gone home, and he headed back to the trailer. He finished up a few reports, gathered his coat, put his phone in his pocket, and headed out to his truck.

Just as he opened the door to his truck, the door on the trailer slammed.

John turned around and looked. The lights were off. The site was empty.

He walked back up the steps and opened the door.

That was when he was hit from behind. His head spun as he fell to the ground.

He couldn't keep his eyes open. He couldn't stand up.

Whoever had hit him was pulling things out of his pocket. A moment later, he heard his truck drive away, but the world was fading to black.

CHAPTER TWENTY-THREE

Arianna and Regan had managed, between the two of them, to make spaghetti. Arianna couldn't imagine juggling two little boys could be so much work, but now she knew.

Just as she carried Tyler to the sink to wash him up, the doorbell rang.

"Maybe that's John. I haven't heard from him all day."

Regan started for the door. "With Zach gone, he's probably been busier."

Arianna went about cleaning up Tyler and was surprised when it was Madeline and Clara's voices she heard.

Madeline walked through the kitchen first. "Oh, it looks like he enjoyed his dinner."

"Yes, and making a mess of his auntie." Arianna acknowledged the red stain on her shirt. "He's lucky I love him so much."

Tyler leaned into her and rested his head on her shoulder. John was lucky she had any love left to spare on him. The children in her life sure had her heart.

Arianna finished washing down Tyler's face and then set him on the floor. "What are you two doing here?"

"John texted me and said he had something he wanted you guys to see at the theater. So I thought I'd drop Clara off with you and stay and watch the boys so Regan could go with you."

Arianna narrowed her eyes on her sister-in-law. "He texted you?"

"Yes." Madeline pulled her phone out of her pocket and showed it to her. "About forty-five minutes ago."

At that moment Arianna's phone buzzed in her pocket. MEET ME AT THE THEATER. I HAVE SOMETHING TO SHOW YOU.

She laughed. "He knew it would take you this long to get here."

Madeline nodded. "I suppose."

Within a half hour the three of them were in the car, and Madeline and Tyler waved goodbye from the front door.

Regan sunk into the seat. "I'm beat."

"You do that every day?" Arianna asked as she pulled out onto the main road.

"Every day."

"Hats off to you, sister. I'm exhausted just having helped."

Regan's eyes were closed before they hit the highway.

Arianna looked in the back seat at Clara. "I have some music from *Annie*. Want to listen?"

Clara smiled and nodded.

Arianna turned on the music, and the two of them sang all the way into town.

All of the lights were on in the theater when they pulled up. Arianna had never seen it look so welcoming.

She parked the car around the back, next to John's truck.

"I wonder what he's up to?"

Regan rubbed her eyes and shrugged. "Got me, Sis. He didn't let me in on this little secret."

The three of them climbed out of the car and started up the back steps. Just as the back door opened, Arianna's phone buzzed in her pocket again.

It was a text message from John.

GOTCHA!

They walked inside, and the door slammed behind them.

She turned around quickly, but there was no one there.

Clara had already moved out onto the stage where the lights were on.

"Auntie, this is wonderful!" She spun in a circle, and Arianna and Regan walked toward her.

Then the lights went dark and a spotlight turned on, shining right on Clara.

Arianna moved toward her. "John, what are you doing? This is scaring me."

Her phone buzzed again. She quickly looked at it.

It was a picture. She moved it closer to look at it. It was a picture of John lying on the ground with his head bleeding.

Arianna's heart pounded in her chest. She reached for Clara, but the lights went dark and Clara wasn't in her reach.

"Bastard, what are you doing? What did you do to John? Where is Clara? Clara!"

Regan reached out in the dark and grabbed hold of Arianna's arm.

"It's Alex. I know it is. I can smell his cologne."

Regan's breath was rapid, and Arianna put her arm around her. She could feel her shake.

"Hamilton, is that you?"

Clara screamed. Both Arianna and Regan moved to the center of the stage, but in the dark, they couldn't risk falling over the side.

Regan clung to her. "What is that smell?"

Arianna sniffed the air. "Smoke."

She turned to see the curtain on the side of the stage illuminate. The flames grew quickly and shot up through the fabric.

"Damn it! We have to get to Clara."

"Now you will all die!" the wicked voice called over from the side of the theater.

Regan broke free from Arianna. "Why are you doing this?"

"I wanted you dead. You and your brother lied to me."

"You didn't want me. You didn't want our baby!" Regan screamed at him in the dark.

Arianna moved in behind her. Alexander Hamilton's figure was now shadowed by the flames.

"By the end of the night, you'll all be dead!" He shouted back, but his shadow was gone. He'd moved, and they could no longer see him.

Arianna's phone buzzed in her pocket again. The smoke grew thicker, and she coughed.

It was another text message from John's phone, but this time it was a picture of Curtis's truck smashed into a pole.

Her entire body shook, and tears burned in her eyes.

"We have to find Clara and get out of here."

They heard her scream.

"C'mon, there is a prop room in the back, and I think that's where she is."

The fire had engulfed the entire side of the stage and was traveling across the top beam. Arianna used the light from the fire to guide her way. The door that led out of the theater was blocked. They'd have to make their way to the front to escape.

The smoke grew thicker, and they both covered their mouths and noses.

Clara's screams grew louder as they neared the other side of the stage. Arianna held up her phone to light the way. She could see the door. It had been blocked by miscellaneous building materials.

She and Regan began to pull the wood and boxes from the door. The curtain on the side of the stage crashed to the ground, and the wood beneath them began to creak.

"We've got to get out of here," Regan cried.

"Clara! Move from the door. I'm going to kick it in!" she yelled through the noise of the stage cracking beneath them.

Sweat began to bead on her neck as she lifted her leg and kicked in the old, wooden door.

Clara climbed over the pile of debris and into her aunt's arms.

Arianna reached for Regan. "Don't you breathe in this air. You have two boys to get home to."

She grabbed her arm, and the three of them ran down the far side of the stage and up through the theater.

When they got to the doors, Arianna turned as she heard the entire curtain crash to the stage. The flames began to roll over the ceiling. She knew they only had a few minutes before they were all dead.

She pushed through the door and shoved Clara into the lobby. Arianna turned to reach for Regan, but she wasn't there.

As she took a step to look for her, she was grabbed and an arm came around her throat.

"She's dead. Now it's your turn." The voice whispered in her ear.

"I've done nothing to you."

"You're whole family will die tonight."

Arianna saw Clara on the floor. "What did you do to her?"

"Tell me what they did to my baby."

"What they did? They gave her to a family who would love her. You tried to kill her."

"And I still will. No one gets away with this."

Arianna felt the cold sting of metal push up against her throat. This wasn't how she wanted to die. She wasn't going to die.

She reached down to her side. Her purse was still draped over her. She felt for her gun, but it was gone.

"Let her go!"

It was Regan's voice, but she couldn't see her in the smoke. Alexander Hamilton's hold around her neck was tighter. If she didn't get out of his grasp, she was going to suffocate.

She could hear Clara behind her. She was alive.

"I said let her go!" Regan shouted again.

"When you're dead, I'll let her go and she can die right here with you."

"Arianna!"

She tried to focus on her sister's voice.

"Dad taught us about fire."

Arianna sucked in a breath, and it burned her lungs. She wanted to cough, but his grip was too tight.

"Do you remember what you were supposed to do in a fire?"

Arianna tried to think. Her world was growing dark, but she struggled to be coherent.

"Do you remember?" Regan shouted again.

Arianna cleared her mind. He used to teach them to stop, drop, and roll. She knew if she let her body go loose, she'd slide from his grip and fall to the floor. Then she could roll away.

But what was Regan going to do? What could…her gun! Regan had her gun!

"One." She heard Regan's voice grow closer. "Two." She'd taken another step. "Three."

Arianna let her body become fluid, and she dropped out of Alexander's arms. The knife scraped against her cheek as she fell to the floor and rolled away. At that moment an explosion ripped through the smoky air, and the man who had held her captive fell down to the ground next to her—lifeless.

Regan hurried to her and grabbed her arm as the flames around them began to move in.

Arianna struggled to her knees and over to Clara.

He'd hit her on the head, but her eyes were open. Blood dripped from above her eyebrow.

"Can you walk?" Arianna shouted against the sound of cracking wood.

Clara stood up and Arianna followed. Just as they pushed open the doors to the theater, they could hear the sounds of sirens coming around the corner.

The three of them made it to the street before the entire roof of the theater caved in.

CHAPTER TWENTY-FOUR

Arianna woke up in a hospital bed. She hadn't remembered getting there.

"Honey, are you okay?"

It was John's voice.

Arianna turned her head. He was next to her in a chair, holding her hand.

She tried to sit up, but she couldn't. Her eyes burned. She took a breath, and her chest ached. It was then she realized she had an oxygen mask on her face.

She lifted her arm to remove it, but she couldn't find the strength. John stood and sat down on the edge of her bed.

Arianna was comforted by that. She'd been afraid something worse had happened to him.

"I'm glad you're okay," he said softly.

She couldn't see his face clearly, but she could hear the tears.

As well as she could, she motioned for him to take the mask off of her.

"You're okay?" Her voice was raspy, only a whisper.

"I'm fine. I have a few staples in the back of my head."

"Curtis?"

She felt another set of hands on her leg. "I'm right here. The son-of-a-bitch stole my truck and wrecked it while I was in surgery. Simone and Avery are okay, too."

Arianna nodded.

"Regan?"

John brushed her hair from her forehead. "She's in the other room. Zach is in there with her. Your mom is in the waiting room with the boys."

"Clara?" The tears came when she asked.

John brushed them away. "She's fine. They have her sucking back some oxygen, and she has a big bandage on her forehead. Nothing more than a scrape. Madeline, Carlos, and the boys are with her."

John placed the oxygen back on her face, and Curtis moved closer to her.

"You have stitches in your cheek. You got cut pretty bad," he told her.

She nodded.

"They confirmed that Hamilton is dead."

She knew that, but it didn't bring her any peace.

Curtis looked at John. "I'm going to go tell Mom and Dad she's awake." He left the room and she noticed John's head fall and tears roll from his cheeks.

"The theater is a complete loss. I knew I'd lost you." He wiped his eyes. "I've never felt pain like that before."

Arianna finally moved her arm and pulled the mask from her face. "I'm here. Everything is okay."

He nodded. "They gave me this." He pulled her ring from his pocket. "I'll give it back to you when you're not all bandaged up."

She looked down at her hands. There were cuts and bandages over her hands and arms.

John bit down on his lip and took a deep breath. "I guess we rebuild?"

She nodded. "Bigger and better."

He laughed through his tears. "That's my girl."

"I need a vacation."

"I think we should extend our trip to San Francisco. Where else do you want to go?"

Arianna closed her eyes and opened them slowly. She could see him more clearly now. "Back to New York as newlyweds."

His mouth had dropped open and then formed into that sexy smile she'd fallen in love with.

"Newlyweds?"

"When you give me that ring back, it better come with an offer to change my name."

"You're sure?"

She nodded and blinked her eyes with heavy lids. When she opened them again, he was smiling wide.

"I'll take that deal."

She smiled. "I guess my days being center stage are over. No one wants an actress with a huge scar across her cheek."

John leaned in and kissed her forehead. "You'll always be my star, and our life together will be your center stage."

I hope you enjoyed Arianna and John's story in Center Stage. Please join us for a preview of Eduardo Keller's story—

Lost and Found

Available May 2013

CHAPTER ONE

Ed Keller leaned back in his chair and kicked his feet up on his desk. The view from his office would never cease to amaze him. The view from his uncle's office was much more spectacular, but he had no reason to complain.

Who would have thought, nearly twenty years ago when he'd asked for an after-school job to afford a limo ride to take a girl to prom, that he'd end up with the title Vice President on his business cards?

He laughed. He couldn't even think of the girl's name that had squeezed at his heart. She'd been older. That he'd remembered. But he'd never done well with older women.

Now he sat atop an empire that his uncle's grandfather had started and his uncle's father had carried on. But it was Zach Benson who made it what it was today.

Benson, Benson, and Hart built big—built on time— and built under budget. Nothing had changed.

Ed didn't have a foreman like Zach had. His other uncle, John Forrester, had been the best foreman any company could have asked for. A loyal employee until Ed's Aunt Arianna made him retire only two years earlier. But another would come along. Right now he had to focus on a new assistant.

Interviewing people for a position shouldn't be an issue. He'd been doing it for years. But a personal assistant had to be in your business, and he didn't like that.

He'd fought it for years. Temps were good. They came, did the work, and left. He figured it was kind of like dating the wrong girl. There weren't any he wanted to spend his life with.

Perhaps his expectations were too high. After all, his Aunt Regan had been Zach's assistant. They'd been married nearly twenty-five years, and she still took care of him. It wouldn't be long before Tyler and Spencer, their sons, would be sitting in Ed's seat.

Ed dropped his feet to the floor and pushed up from his chair. When the time was right, he'd find the assistant of his dreams. He'd given up on the woman of his dreams, so an assistant would have to do.

He walked to the elevator and pressed the button to go down to the lobby. There was a Starbucks there now, and he'd grown very fond of caramel lattes, thanks to his Aunt Arianna, though he didn't go for the skinny version. His Uncle John would say it was a bit too frilly a drink for a man in the construction business. His Uncle Zach, on the other hand, would argue that it was a good stress reliever.

Ed laughed at himself. What an eclectic bunch of people he had in his family. And even without them there with him, he still enjoyed them.

The gathering of the masses in the Starbucks also entertained him, almost as much as the thoughts of his family and their differences.

Ed ordered his drink and stood at the counter waiting for it to be handed to him.

He could look around the store, spot and name each kind of person. There was the tourist, the executive, and the assistant. There was couple, obviously just downtown for the day and…hmmm, one that stumped him.

She was professional, probably interviewing by the way she was dressed, but she wasn't comfortable with the big building and the mass of people. She was using Starbucks as a common ground, something familiar, to ease her nerves.

He listened as she ordered her drink—decaf and nonfat. What fun was in that, he wondered.

She tucked her change back into her purse and walked to the end of the counter to wait for her drink next to Ed.

Flowery perfume filled his nose. She had a sweet side.

The lady behind the counter handed Ed his iced caramel latte. He turned to leave and, he'd say so himself, that was when things got interesting.

The woman who had been standing behind him, searching in her bag for something, looked up just as Ed turned around. She shifted to move out of his way, but instead she moved right into him.

Ed's hands slipped from the condensation on the cup, and the entire, cold drink poured down the front of the woman.

She let out a stifled scream, and her hands went into the air. "Oh-my-God!"

"I'm very sorry."

Ed turned toward the counter and grabbed a handful of napkins. He would have helped to mop up her clothes, but he noticed that the white silk shirt clung to her and decided it just wasn't a good idea to try.

"Look what you did!" She ripped the napkins from his hand and began to blot away the coffee which had already stained the shirt.

"Sorry, but I think you ran into me."

She snapped her head up again. "Oh, men. You're not always right, you know. Sometimes you do make mistakes."

Not only was she not as sweet as her flowery perfume, she was jaded. Bad news.

"Again, I'm very sorry. How can I help you?" He turned and reached for more napkins, but when she pulled them from his hand, he noticed she was crying.

"I think you've done enough."

"I still think I can help in some way."

"Listen. My suit is ruined. This is the only one I have. I was searching for a job, and I can't do that now. I can't hand out resumes looking like this."

Ed watched as the woman continued to wipe off her blouse, but to no avail. It was ruined, but he still wasn't going to take the blame.

"Are you looking for a job in this building?"

She let out a grunt. "Why else would I be here?"

"I was just asking. I know most of the businesses in the building. Perhaps I can help you out."

The woman pursed her lips. "I don't need your charity."

"It's not charity. You seem to be in need of a job, and I'm sure I can help you find one."

"What, do you own this place?" She waved her arms in the air.

"Let me see your resume."

The woman stared at him as if he'd lost his mind. That wasn't new. You didn't run a multi-million dollar company in your mid-thirties without people giving you a shifty eye.

Her coffee was set on the counter. He moved in to grab it, but she moved quicker. "I'll get this. I can't afford to waste a sip of this. It's my breakfast and lunch."

She picked up the coffee and moved to a table where she set down the cup and pulled a resume from her bag. She handed it to Ed. "Here it is. I hate to say it, but I'm desperate. If I don't find a job in three days, I have to go home."

"Why? Does that suit turn back into a pumpkin and your glass slipper breaks?"

"Have you ever been desperate for anything in your life?"

He didn't have anything to say. The only desperate thing he'd ever done was ask his uncle for a job at fifteen so he could get that limo to prom. Look where it landed him twenty years later. She was right. He'd never been desperate for anything.

"How do you feel about assistant work for a commercial builder?"

"You actually know of a job?"

"I actually know of a job." He folded her resume and tucked it into his pocket. "Ed Keller is an executive at Benson, Benson, and Hart. He needs an assistant."

Her face went pale, and her lips parted. This reaction went past him spilling his drink on her. "That was the business I was going to leave my resume with."

"You're into architecture?"

He watched as she swallowed hard, but the color hadn't returned to her cheeks yet. "Not exactly, but you think you can get me in there?"

"I'm sure I can."

She nodded and picked up her coffee. "You don't think Mr. Keller will mind my attire?"

Ed smiled. "I guarantee he will be fine. Your resume is impressive. I'm sure that he'd understand that accidents happen."

She nodded again, nervously. "I'm still mad that you ruined my suit."

"And I'm sorry that you bumped into me. But if you'll come with me, I'll get you a job. And, if you're hungry for lunch later, there is a hot dog cart out back. I'd love to buy you some lunch."

Darcy watched the elevator doors close. She was alone with the man who had ruined her day, but also had offered her an opportunity. She was scared to death.

She'd planned this day for so long. Now she was in the building, and she was headed to the company offices of Benson, Benson, and Hart.

Her heart pounded in her chest. She hadn't expected this. It was in her plans, but as the doors opened to the floor and the name was before her on the wall in big, shiny letters, she thought she might just throw up.

She only knew one thing about herself—her past—and it had led her to Benson, Benson, and Hart. She'd planned to attempt to, at least, get in the door since all the other jobs she'd applied for had fallen through. The journey to find out about herself wasn't supposed to drop her in the office where she knew her all her answers would lie. This was supposed to be months down the road when she'd had time to explore more about herself and where she'd come from. Now what?

The man exited the elevator and looked at her. "Are you coming?"

"I seem to be very nervous."

He reached for her hand and pulled her gently from the elevator. He took off his suit coat and draped it over her shoulders. It was a courteous move to hide her huge stained blouse, which she knew she'd caused because she wasn't paying attention, but she still wasn't going to let him think he didn't do it. Men would use you if you weren't careful.

The man led her to an office, and the name on the door read EDUARDO KELLER. She sucked in a breath as he opened the door and walked in.

"Have a seat." He pointed to the chairs in front of the desk.

Darcy took a seat, set her bag to the side, and then slid her arms through the sleeves of the jacket he'd draped on her. She probably looked ridiculous. He was at least six feet tall and broad shouldered. She wasn't very tall at all, and she didn't even come close to filling out the jacket.

The man sat behind the desk and turned on the computer monitor.

"Should you be doing that," she asked?

"I need to find the application information to fill out for the human resource department."

"You're going to fill it out?"

"I usually do when I'm hiring people."

She looked around the office. Eduardo Keller had no personal affects. The man must be all business.

"Why are you doing the hiring?"

The man stopped what he was doing. He folded his hands on the top of the desk and gazed at her with dark brown eyes.

"Because I'm Ed Keller."

Ed had seen his share of angry women in his life. When this woman's face turned the color of Santa's suit, he knew he'd crossed the line.

She stood from the chair and grabbed her bag. "Do you think this is funny? You're messing with my life."

"Whoa." He stood from his seat. "Calm down."

"Calm down? I will not calm down."

"I've seen your resume. You're very qualified for the position I need to fill, and I'd like to help you."

"Help me?" She lifted the bag onto her shoulder. "Help me? Why would you want to do that? You're just some stuck up executive who can play with people, like spilling coffee on a woman to get her into your office. Is this what you do here?"

Ed planted his hands firmly on his desk and looked at her. "You told me you had three days to find a job. You told me I ruined all your chances by messing up your blouse. So you can either hear me out, or you can leave here with your stained clothing, your wrinkled resume, and your bad attitude and find a job."

The woman sucked in a breath and let it out slowly. "What is the job?"

"Executive assistant."

"To you?"

"Yes."

Her shoulders dropped, and she bit her bottom lip. She was contemplating, but he didn't know, in his own heart, which way he wanted her to go now. It was very likely he'd just made a big mistake offering it to her if she was so volatile.

The woman set her bag back on the ground and extended her hand to him. "Darcy McCary, your new assistant."

Darcy studied Eduardo Keller as he shook her hand. Was he happy? Mad? Oh, he'd been messing with her, and now she really felt stupid. But she needed the job, and he was right—she was very qualified. She needed to find an apartment and establish some savings. Private investigators hadn't been cheap, and she couldn't tell her father that she'd hired them.

She had a debt to pay and a life to understand—her life.

Darcy McCary was in Tennessee to find her birth mother, and the investigator told her that all ties led to Nashville and to Benson, Benson, and Hart.

MEET THE AUTHOR

 Bernadette Marie has been an avid writer since the early age of 13, when she'd fill notebook after notebook with stories that she'd share with her friends. Her journey into novel writing started the summer before eighth grade when her father gave her an old typewriter. At all times of the day and night you would find her on the back porch penning her first work, which she would continue to write for the next 22 years.

In 2007 – after marriage, filling her chronic entrepreneurial needs, and having five children – Bernadette began to write seriously with the goal of being published. That year she wrote 12 books. In 2009 she was contracted for her first trilogy and the published author was born. In 2011 she (being the entrepreneur that she is) opened her own publishing house, 5 Prince Publishing, and has released contemporary titles and began the process of taking on other authors in other genres.

In 2012 Bernadette Marie found herself on the bestsellers lists of iTunes and Amazon to name a few. Her office wall is lined with colorful Post It notes with the titles of books she will be releasing in the very near future, with hope that they too will grace the bestsellers lists.

Bernadette spends most of her free time driving her kids to their many events. She is also an accomplished martial artist who earned her conditional second degree black belt in Tang Soo Do in October 2012. An avid reader, she enjoys most, the works of Nora Roberts, Karen White, and Megan Hart, to name a few. She loves to meet readers who enjoy reading contemporary romances and she always promises Happily Ever After.

Made in the USA
Lexington, KY
04 November 2013